Carmen's Destiny
The Doorways

By DJ L. Bajraktari

First edition

ISBN: 979-8-3482-0906-3 (Paperback)

Cover art by Dj Bajraktari and Robyn Bajraktari
Editing by Robyn Bajraktari and Sandra P.B (Sanpan)
Proofreading by Robyn Bajraktari
.

Acknowledgment

A Special Thanks for more significant support:

I want to thank everyone who has supported me along this journey of becoming a published author.

I have struggled to find the proper guidance and support since I started writing this book at 12. At 16, I reworked the book in hopes of better support and encouragement, which I did not find. Now, at 31, I get to live out my dream. My loving wife and children have supported and encouraged me to be creative and write with passion. I have more ideas for this storyline, as well as for other book series and short stories.

Contents

Back Cover Excerpt

Destiny is believed to be an unknown path in life. A path that shifts and changes with the choices you make. You never know when something exceptional or treacherous will happen to your hopeful plan.

Each person holds the power to make their own choices and mold the path ahead. However, there are those who, on their own path, can change or end yours instantly. What if there was a force, a being, that wanted to allow everyone a fair opportunity in life or could take those choices away altogether? Without destiny, life itself wouldn't exist. Destiny is not only the path in a person's life, it is the story of a person's past, present, and future. We should all take care and think through our actions and choices responsibly. Destiny can only be written once, or can it?

Embark on a journey with Carmen as he faces his destiny. He will face life-changing discoveries of his family's past as he tries to prove himself fit to become the next king and gain control of his powers. Carmen stumbles upon unknown dangers and challenges when he breaks the rules and accidentally falls into another universe. The journey home will not be easy. Riddled with danger and secrets, Carmen will have to push his capabilities to the limits and seek help from unknown sources or risk the future he was destined to have.

Prologue

Many years ago, in the 13th century, a man named Domonic Remy from the village of Narata believed he possessed the power to travel between different universes. As a child, he was raised by two abusive parents and often found himself locked in the basement as punishment. He would sit on the floor to meditate and think of a happy place to help ease his pains. Now and then, he would find himself transported to these other universes. They were no longer dreams; they were real. Most of his time was spent traveling these universes and learning their secrets. It was an excellent way for him to escape the pain. Domonic was often punished for his disappearances from the basement. This gave him more time and ambition to practice his abilities. The only thing that kept him returning to his universe was his love for Deniha, who he would one day make his wife.

Over time, he began to realize that by traveling to these universes, he could control time, space, and everyone's destiny; he could influence one's choices in life, changing their fate. He did not wish to use this ability on others maliciously but extend it to help improve their quality of life. If others in the village could share this great power, they would be granted control over their destiny. Ultimately, Domonic could not prove his abilities were stronger and more advanced than the others in the village, as he could not take anyone with him to these other universes. Village folk mocked him. He became a disgrace to his community. If appropriately trained, everyone in the village could possess the power of energy and the elements. A select few could go invisible and teleport, but it was rare. When Domonic tried to showcase his abilities, some thought he went invisible, and others thought it was just a teleportation trick. Many thought there was no way one individual could possess such power. Even Domonic's now-pregnant wife, Deniha, shut him out to avoid ridicule from others in the village, forcing Domonic to leave the village in search of a new home.

After traveling for many days and nights, Domonic grew frail. He needed to find a place to sleep, a place to eat, somewhere he could call home. With his last bit of energy, he planted his feet on the ground, took a deep breath, and began whirling his hands from side to side, causing the trees to bend and wrap around each other. The leaves fluttered and shook as they whipped around with the branches. Quickly, a small hut formed, and a slight glow came from within. Panting out of breath, Domonic carefully peeled back a layer of bark off a tree and stuck it in the opening to create a door. Pleased with his tiny home, he collapsed to the floor from exhaustion.

Hours passed before Domonic woke again. He was overwhelmed with hunger. Knowing he needed to find food, he looked out between the branches, but all he could see was darkness; finding food now would be near impossible. But with a loud, painful grumble in his stomach, he knew he had to try. He leaned forward to push open his makeshift door; he imagined walking out onto fields of fruits and vegetables. Suddenly, Domonic sees a light peeking through the door. He excitedly gives the door a shove, shocked in disbelief; he stands there momentarily, peering out the door.

In the opening of the doorway, bright colors of reds, greens, and yellows swirl together in a mesmerizing twist. Slowly, the colorful vortex opens from the center, revealing a blinding sunlight. As Domonic's eyes adjusted to the light, he saw fields of apples, pears, bananas, and cherry trees. He glances back at the wall of branches, but no light shines; he just sees the darkness of night. He crawls out to the nearest apple tree, quickly ripping down the reddest apple he had ever seen. Viciously, he bit into the apple, ripping out big chucks and gulping them down. He couldn't believe the taste; it was so sweet and juicy. He collected all the fruit he could hold and rushed back into his hut to feast. He pulled the door shut to eat in peace as he wasn't sure what was lurking in the shadows of this world. As he ate, an idea popped into his head. He leaned forward, putting his hand to the door. He imagined one of the other universes he'd visited. He focused all his intentions on the door. Just like before, light shined through the cracks of the door. He gave it a push. His eyes widened as he saw the vortex of purple and green swirling together. He began laughing hysterically as he realized he had just found a way to prove his power to others. He smiled big, thinking about going home again; he could be welcomed back with open arms and be a hero! He could be with his one true love again!

Upon arriving home, Domonic was not welcomed with open arms as he had hoped. No one even bothered glancing in his direction. But this didn't matter to him as he was determined to prove his abilities. He went straight to the edge of the village where a large meadow sat bordered by trees on the other side. Aside from a few children playing or cows grazing, this area was never used. First, he began marking out 21 medium-sized rectangular holes in a large circular pattern, pouring a mixture of clay, straw, and crushed stone into each one to create a solid slab. This caught the attention of the village folk. They watched and scoffed as he worked day in and day out. Domonic kept busy as he eagerly worked on his grand plan. Their comments weren't going to break his spirits; they were finally going to see his power. The teasing and ridicule would cease, turning to joy and love.

As each slab cured and hardened, Domonic began building abnormally large doors. Each was unique in its way. Some were strange and ugly with little effort, while others were beautiful with outstanding craftsmanship. Villagers gathered each day as if watching a show. Their murmurs of disgust slowly turned to murmurs of curiosity. No one understood what Domonic was building or why, but they felt a strange sense of safety. A select few were insistent that Domonic was up to no good and needed to be stopped, or they all would be doomed.

In just a few months, Domonic completed all 21 doors. This was enough to open a pathway to the most essential universes he had visited. He called out to the crowd of people mesmerized by his work.

"Today marks a glorious day in history. Today is the day we can all visit wonderful new universes. Some of these universes will challenge us, others will help us to end hunger and illness. In some universes, time is nonexistent, and in others, when you leave, you have gone back in time, undoing what has previously been done."

Everyone groaned and sighed. This was not the excitement they were expecting out of his creation. Some booed and mocked him, claiming he had just gone mad and should be locked up. Others just walked away in disgust. Domonic ran into the middle of the circle in a last-ditch effort to stop people from leaving. He raised his hand up high into the sky, his fingers began to twitch and wiggle, his eyes fluttered, and his face contorted as if he was struck with pain. The wind started whipping and whirling. People ran, screaming in terror of what was happening before their eyes. Thick gray clouds rolled in quickly as the wind picked up faster than any storm they had seen. Thunder roared with loud booms, shaking the ground violently. Suddenly, a lightning bolt shot down from the sky, striking Domonic, he smiled as he felt the current run through him. Quickly, he spun, pointing at each door. Electricity shot from his fingers connecting with each door, causing them to glow light blue. Everyone screamed, running in horror to take shelter.

With a quick motion, Domonic flung his hands
back up to the sky, sending all electrical
currents with it. Just like that, it was over. The
clouds began to clear, revealing the sunlight as
the wind calmed to a breeze. No one dared
approach Domonic in fear for their lives as
they remained cowering from all the
commotion.

"Please don't be afraid," Domonic begs. "This
is what I have been trying to show you. New
universes that could change all of our lives."
The crowd of people was unmoved except for
one. Deniha slowly worked her way through the
crowd. Her face was calm and soft. She lay one
hand on the lump of her belly, the other on her
back for support. As she approached him, she
placed a hand on his cheek and just stared at
him. Her soft lips pressed together as she
lovingly gazed into his ocean-blue eyes. She
had always loved his eyes; they were like
drifting away in the calm seas.

"I am so sorry I ever doubted you, my love.
Please forgive us. We are now listening to you."
Her voice was soft and angelic. Domonic
smoothly swept a piece of her hair from her

face. He smiled as he leaned in to gently kiss her forehead. They held this position for a long time. This was all Domonic needed, her. Everything he did was for her and their child. He loved her more than anything on earth; to have her acceptance was everything.

Eventually, he backed away, not breaking eye contact with her. Watching her lovingly, he slowly walked to one of his favorite doors. He had put a lot of detail into this one. It was extensive, with an arch peeking to a point at the top. The molding around the edges was carved and painted with a variety of fruits and vegetables, all connected with leafy vines that wrapped all the way down to the wooden knob forged from a stump.

Deniha nodded to him, signaling for him to open the door. With one smooth motion, he turned the knob and gave the door a hard shove. The wooden door creaked, revealing the familiar vortex. The crowd had grown quiet; only slight gasps could be heard throughout. Everyone was in awe, watching the red, green, and yellow hues swirl together. The villagers' gasps turned to loud murmurs of amazement as the vortex opened completely, revealing the new universe on the other side of the door.

"Friends and family, you may never go hungry again. This is just the beginning. There are more universes like this one with lots to offer and teach us. The 21 doorways I have created here for you are just some of many I have seen." The words *friends and family* struck the crowd. You could feel the guilt wash over them. For years, they had been so unkind to him, shutting him out, and still, he managed to maintain his love and faith in the people around him. Days went by, and the village created a system. Teams were sent through particular doors to collect supplies. These supplies ranged from foods; to herbs and plants for medicine; and metals for forging. The teams were broken into groups of 8 people. They lost a few foragers in the beginning days and didn't want to risk losing more family or friends. Two people stood to watch at the door, one inside and one outside, to ensure the door was never accidentally shut while anyone was inside, as the vortex never opened in the same place twice. The other six villagers entered the door to forge with a rope tied around their waist. The rule was made that no one was

allowed to go further than the rope permitted after a few people got lost from wandering too far and never found their way back. Everything seemed great for a while. Villagers no longer had to suffer; hunger was abolished, and illnesses were reduced now that they had plenty of herbs to help heal and cure ailments. Domonic had become the hero he had hoped and dreamed about. Little did he know his glory was coming to a quick end.

The doors had been active for a month now with many successful explorations of these new worlds. There had been a few folks who claimed to see shadows. Still, the claims were quickly dismissed as nothing had been found by any groups sent out to investigate these odd occurrences. All the doors had been checked for signs of life, but they seemed utterly empty. A few weeks later, a loud scream echoed through the field as everyone was about to turn in for the day. Everyone frantically looked around to locate where the sound came from. In front of one of the doors, a man lay on the ground, his chest pierced with a spear. A woman lay over his lifeless body sobbing. She quickly looked up to yell something as a second spear flew out of the door, piercing her face. Her body slumped to the ground motionless. No one moved out of pure fear. Who or what was attacking, and where did they come from? Domonic sprang into action, running towards the door to slam it shut. Just as he reached the door, a long bluish-gray dragon flew out. Hovering over the circle of doors, it let out a loud screeching roar, causing everyone to cover their ears in pain. Fire shot out, lighting the evening sky as the roar thundered on.

The Dragon scanned the ground, looking at all the people cowering in fear. Guards from the village charged the field, shouting and hollering. Their fist clenched as they used their powers to hurl giant chunks of earth in the Dragon's direction. Unfazed, the Dragon just let the earth chunks crash into its body and crumble to the ground. This only angered the beast more. It pulled back its head and began shooting fireballs at the guards. Their bodies dropped to the ground as their searing flesh bubbled off their bones. Letting out another blood-curdling roar, the Dragon looked towards the open door. An army of enraged, screaming men and women charged out the door as if signaled by the Dragon. The villagers jumped up from the ground as adrenaline ran rampant in their hearts, turning fear into fighting fury. Energy balls were hurled back and forth between the opposing forces. Bodies dropped to the ground left and right as the two sides brawled it out.

Suddenly, Domonic saw an opportunity; just a few steps away from him was the door of time. If he could reach the inside, he could turn back time and shut the doors before the Dragon and army rushed out. He made a leap for it and yanked the door open. A fireball caught the back of his leg, causing him to fall and roll through the door. He stumbled across the ground as a green aura radiated around his body. He sat up quickly, crossing his legs to meditate as he closed his eyes and took a deep breath. His body began to levitate off the ground; a low, soft hum rumbled out of his mouth as his eyes shot open, now glowing green. Tilting forward, he flew towards the door's opening and into the open field. He flew through the air until he sat in the sky above the center of all 21 doors with his hands on his knees, palms facing the sky. Everything froze in place; turning his palms upside down, the Dragon and the army began to fade away into nothing. Domonic uncrossed his legs and slowly sank to the ground; the green aura dissipated from his body on his descent. Everyone scattered around, slamming doors shut to avoid another attack. Bodies of those who perished during the attack still lay on the ground, lifeless. Domonic dropped to his knees, despair heavy in his ocean-blue eyes; what went wrong they should have been brought back. Time should have been completely undone. Was he not strong enough, or was destiny keeping the victims it had already claimed? Even the dead bodies from the attacking army remained.

Those who survived angrily glared at Domonic. Those who had hidden away in their homes for safety began to emerge. Screams and cries are heard across the village as they discover the massacre of friends and family before them. Anger and resentment grew exponentially more towards Domonic as the blood of their loved ones soaked into the ground. They blamed him for this unfortunate event. This tragedy wouldn't have occurred if it weren't for his creation.

"KILL HIM!" one man belted from the crowd. Everyone marched towards Domonic, their hands out, charged with power. Domonic begged and pleaded with the angry mob. He tried to form an energy field to protect himself. But suddenly, a woman's shout pierces through him, stealing his concentration as her words fill his heart with fear.

"Kill his wife too! She's pregnant with his offspring, and we don't need any more of his kind!" she screamed to the crowd. Domonic charged in the direction of his family home to save his wife, only to be struck back by a fireball. Pain shot through his shoulder, but he needed to get to Deniha. Domonic stumbles forward again, getting hit by fireballs repeatedly. His skin was burning as he cried out for mercy, crumpling to the ground. Looking through the window of their home, Deniha felt powerless as she cried. She watched Domonic take multiple devastating hits. Being pregnant stunted Denihas powers. She wanted to protect her husband, but she would be of no help to him and only put herself and their child's life in harm's way if she tried to intervene. So she wiped the tears from her face and blew a kiss in Domonic's direction. Regret about what she was about to do washed over her as the reality of what she had to do set in.

"Goodbye, my sweet love, I have to protect our child. I will make sure it lives on in your honor," she whispered as she turned and ran for the back door. She had to do whatever she could for the safety of their child. She snatched a bag full of apples before running out the door. She stumbled as she pulled a shawl over her head to cover her face and hair. Her black bangs stuck out as she wasted no time trying to stuff the tiny pieces in. She ran in a low crouch, trying to be as quiet as possible, with one hand cradling her stomach as the other slid gently across the smooth stone of the village houses. She continuously looked back for anyone following; she could hear the villagers shouting for her as they kicked in her door, making a loud bang against the stone. She shuddered but continued slithering between houses as quickly and quietly as possible. As she reached the edge of the village,

she pulled up the long ends of her dress so they wouldn't catch on the branches and darted through the woods. The forest was thick and damp as she raced through, ducking under low branches and pushing back shrubs to make her way through. The sounds of angry yelling faded, replaced by her panicked breaths and the snapping of branches as she descended into the abysmal forest. She knew of a kingdom called Zentu, just a three-day journey away. Fear raced through her heart, knowing she would be pregnant and alone in her long journey to safety.

As hours passed, she moved as quickly as she could through the treacherous forest. Sunlight was beginning to fade, but she couldn't stop now with the risk of being captured. Suddenly, A sharp pain shot through her stomach, causing her to clench her stomach to try and push through the pain. Deniha realizes she must sit. She finds a fallen log to rest on momentarily. She breathed heavily, dropping the bag of apples next to her, trying to catch her breath. She pulled the shawl off her head, wiping the tears that filled her eyes as she rubbed her belly.

"Shhh, my sweet angel. I know you're hurting and tired, but Mummy needs to keep moving. I need to make sure you're safe." Her stomach let out a loud rumble, reminding her she hadn't eaten since the night before. "Are you hungry? Is that what this is?" Another rumble went through her stomach as if answering her. Taking an apple from the bag, she couldn't help but think about the fate that befell her beloved Domonic as she stared into the woods around her.

She saw his life leave his eyes, reminded her they could have had more time together if she had supported him more from the start. The half-eaten apple falls from Deniha's hand as crushing sorrow grips her broken heart. Sobbing uncontrollably, Deniha slid off the log to her knees as tears poured from her blue eyes, soaking the moss-covered ground. Collapsing to her side, she lay there cradling the baby within her womb until her sobs became silent tears. Eventually, crying herself to sleep.

She had only been sleeping for a few hours before she felt a slight poking on her arm. She jolted awake, and a tall man stood in what looked like royal garments. His pants were brown, following the shape of his legs. His white silk shirt peeked out from under the medium-length coat with swirling patterns of blue and gold. His sleeves were rolled up his arms to keep cool from the evening's heat. She scrambled backward, afraid he was there to take her back to the village. He knelt slightly and stuck his hands out, showing he meant no harm. Breathing heavily, she stopped scrambling and watched him intently.

"It's ok, my dear. I'm not going to hurt you. I am King Alden Animus. Who might you be, my dear lady? What has brought you out to this dangerous forest?" The King spoke softly. Deniha needed to figure out how to respond. She knew he couldn't discover the truth about what had happened in the village, so she didn't want to tell him her last name. If he had gotten word of her husband, he would surely kill her. She hesitated for a moment, looking for what to say.

"I...... I...... I don't know." she finally responded, stuttering to get the words out. "M....M...my name is Deniha, but I don't remember anything else. Where am I? What's happening to me? How did I get here?" She pretends to question so she doesn't raise suspicion. She spoke softly as if frantically asking herself but loud enough for the King to hear. She lays her hands on her stomach and dramatically screams. "OH MY, AND I THINK I'M WITH CHILD?" The King reaches his hand out caringly to help her up. He offers to take her back to his kingdom, where she can rest and get back to health. She sighed with relief as it seemed her lies had worked.

A few years pass, and Deniha and her son, whom she named Domonic after her late husband, live in the castle with King Alden. With no last name to give to her child, King Alden offered up his last name to Deniha and Domonic. He grew fond of them over the previous few years and considered them family. King Alden and his wife, Queen Isabella, who was barren, looked after them as their kin. This secured them a permanent home within the

Animus castle. Deniha often went for walks with the King's wife, Queen Isabella.

On one of their walks, they noticed a large group of wagons rolling in with large structures on them. They were covered with fabric, but the shape seemed oddly familiar to Deniha. The Queen ushered Deniha back to the castle. She seemed to be in a panic.

"We need to get inside quickly. I forgot the Naratan army was making a delivery today; it's not safe for us right now." Daniha's heart sank as she heard her village name. Panic set in quickly as she kept up a running pace with the Queen. What if someone recognized her? What if they exposed her and Domonic for who they really were? She pulled her shawl over her head and wrapped it around her cheeks to try and hide her face.

The Queen and Daniha went to the kitchen inside the castle for tea. The Queen told Deniha all about this powerful and crazy man who had created doors to other universes and how he started an attack on the village. The village army was forced to kill him and his pregnant wife. Daniha was deeply saddened listening to the Queen speak. Just the thought of her poor husband's death saddened her, but she needed to maintain her composure to not let her secret slip. The Queen told her about all the failed attempts to destroy the doors as they had learned that the creatures and people from within had unknown means to open the doors and enter into their universe. Planks had to be placed on the doors, and they had to be sealed shut to keep things from getting in or out. Some doors were harmless, others caused destruction and chaos. One door causes extreme rage if stationed by it for too long. A meeting had been called by the three World Kingdoms: Narata, Animus, and Zentu. The three kings agreed to divide the doors evenly amongst the kingdoms to keep them out of the villages' safety. The doors King Animus obtained were brought to a large meadow just off the backside of the castle. The trees were extremely thick around the meadow, and there was just a narrow pathway to access it. The meadow could only be seen from the highest point in the castle over the treetops. Deniah watched the doors every night before falling asleep; they reminded her of her beloved

Domonic. After a few months of organization, a large monument was built over the doors. It took some time for the structure to be completed as the King insisted on only using the most robust materials.

Once the building was complete, Daniha realized the true extent of Domonic's powers. His creations caused fear and panic among the strongest world leaders even after death. He could end the doors and stop the madness if he were still alive. The thought pained her as she missed and loved him dearly. However, she couldn't bear to think of the destruction still being caused by his creation. Her biggest fear was trying to find out if their child had inherited his father's powers. If so, she risks exposing her secret. This would put both Dehiha and Domonic's lives at significant risk. She did everything she could to test little Domonic's powers to see what he could do. Still, he never presented anything out of the ordinary.

On Domonic's 16th Birthday, King Alden and Queen Isabella gave him a unique gift. They wanted him to take over the kingdom when the time was right. However, to do so, he would need to fulfill three commitments. These commitments were to be passed down to other future prospective kings to prove their worthiness. Domonic was beyond excited and accepted his new destiny with open arms. Domonic had grown into a strong, adventurous young man who looked much like his father. Domonic inherited his dark hair and ocean-blue eyes. He always looked at everything with positivity and hopefulness. He was brave and kind and put everyone else before himself. He was going to make an excellent king one day. Deniah was proud of him. He was just like his father in every good and pure way, thankfully without his unique powers. Knowing this made keeping her secret easier. She could live without worry; Domonic and the rest of the kingdom would never need to know the truth. With the doors locked away and protected and her husband's powers gone with his death, everyone could live safely moving forward.

Doorway Discovery

Two hundred years later, the Seven Doors of Domonic, located within the Animus Kingdom, were left in the hands of King Tobias' sixteen-year-old son Carmen Animus. Attempts to destroy the doors were still unsuccessful.

Carmen is not like the other teens in the kingdom. When he was twelve, he presented signs of special powers, unlike anything anyone had ever seen. Everyone can possess powers of the elements, but only Carmen, although not good at it, can levitate. Occasionally, when Carmen tried, he could absorb the energy from an energy ball thrown at him, whereas others could only deflect it. Carmen's Uncle Menius spent much time with him, teaching him how to control his powers and trying to understand these strange powers unknown to the world.

While learning to control his powers, King Tobias must prepare Carmen for his journey to becoming Animus's future King. Generationally, those in line to be King are tasked with three commitments. First is to be part of the rotation of guards standing watch of the Doors of Domonic. Each day, Carmen must dedicate 4 hours to standing guard on his own. This shows he is patient and brave enough to protect the people of Animus. The second is to master one's own powers. A great king must show strength, control, and discipline to command a kingdom and its army. Most people only learn to master one or two of their powers, but a king must be in tune with themself and master all powers. The third is to find true love. It is a strong belief that a king is calmer, sweeter, and more logical with a strong Queen by his side.

Carmen was only a child when he accepted these responsibilities. Still, the time has come to begin his journey to complete his commitments. Carmen has always cared about fulfilling all his promises and obligations. He has no plans to let down his kingdom; one day, he will continue his father's legacy and be known as a great king to all of Animus' people. Carmen longs to fulfill his destiny of being the future King not only in honor of his father but for his mother, who tragically passed during childbirth.

Although he never met her, Carmen's dad spoke of her often, describing her beauty, bravery, and brute strength. She was a woman of the people, and her generosity had no bounds. His father would always remark on how he carried on her dark black hair and her enormous smile that sat under her little nose. He would always laugh at himself and say how glad he was that Carmen didn't end up with his honker of nose.

Carmen has just begun to learn a few basics of his powers: Earth, water, and energy. Air and fire have been a struggle, but Menius always told him to focus on his knowledge and expand. As for his unknown powers, they were random and sporadic at best, making it almost impossible to try mastering them. In all his readings, Menius had never seen anyone mentioned to have powers like Carmens. It doesn't help that Carmen has never been able to recreate them consistently. Menius and King Tobias warn him often to be careful when using his powers out in public and only use them for the kingdom's safety, for lack of control and minimal understanding of his unseen powers could spark panic within the villages.

Carmen tries hard each day to recreate these strange powers and expand on the ones he knows, but he always seems to find them more challenging to control within himself. He continues to struggle with even his elemental powers and can't understand what is wrong with him. He often feels defeated, though he never gives up because he doesn't want to disappoint those counting on him. He must prove he's capable of being a great king, running the kingdom, and maybe even become a hero.

One day, while Carmen is standing guard at the doors, time seems to tick by slowly in the quiet, with each minute feeling like hours. He decides to put the time to good use by practicing honing his powers and trying to figure out how to access the unknown powers he possesses. As he hovers some rocks and flings them into the woods, trying to hit a dangling leaf on a tree, he hears a strange whisper. A woman's voice calls for him like a mother softly calls to her child.

Carmen pokes his head through the monument door. Cautiously, he makes his way around, checking behind each door, searching for the source of the voice. Seeing that he is still alone, he decides the voice must have come from within one of the mysterious universes. Although no one has been reported missing, he fears someone must be trapped behind one of the doors and is trying to get out. Although forbidden, Carmen has always wondered what is located behind the seven doors of Domonic.

He has heard stories of people who went missing while trespassing near the doors, but their bodies were never recovered. Perhaps they just got lost in the woods? What harm could it be just to open and check beyond the doors? Maybe he could save a lost soul.

The first door molding is wrapped with a floral decorative edge. The door itself is painted white with elegant pink flowers. The doorknob is solid gold with vine-like flowers molded into the edges. A sizable thick board lays across the doors, secured by two steel hooks. Many centuries ago, these were placed on all the doors to seal them shut and keep everyone out.

He lifts it off slowly, resting it against the side of the door frame. His hand trembles slightly as he reaches gradually for the knob. Inches away, a flash of orange light sparks between his fingers and the knob, startling him and causing him to jump back. Heart racing, he looks between his hand and the knob curiously before cautiously reaching for the golden knob again. The orange sparks flash between his fingers again, but this time, instead of pulling back, he pushes forward and grabs the knob firmly. He tenses, waiting for stinging pain to assault his hand, but after a moment, he realizes there is no pain. It actually feels warm and welcoming as he turns the knob. It feels like he is warming his hand before a fire on a cold night. Slowly, he pulls on the door, causing it to creak loudly as he opens it just enough to peek inside. All he sees is an empty black space. He gasps as his mind is filled instantly with knowledge of the universe; this is the universe of imagination. Once a person fully enters the door, all their dreams, wishes, and fantasies will come true. This door radiates an unfixable danger if the wrong person ever steps inside. World domination, unlimited wealth, and power can all be obtained from this universe and used for the wrong purpose.

Luckily, Carmen does not see anyone or
hear the whisper coming from inside this door,
so he hastily shuts the door and replaces the
wooden plank, locking the door shut. He has to
be sure to relock the doors as he doesn't want
to unleash something terrible on the kingdom
or have anyone find out he opened the doors.
Carmen then moves on to the next door.

The second door is trimmed with red and
gold. Delicately carved onto this door are
ripples like the surface of water. Carmen
unseals the door quickly as his curiosity to
learn about this universe grows; Surprisingly,
the same orange sparks appear as he touches
the knob. He opens it just enough to fit his
head through, leaving the rest of his body in
the real world so he doesn't accidentally get
trapped within. This universe is filled with
pictures and paintings of plants and empty
skies. He wonders why there are no people in
the photographs or paintings. His
disappointment grows, knowing he can never
ask anyone about what he is seeing, as it would

reveal he opened the door. He thinks for a second, remembering that at the first door, everything he needed to know came to him, and he wondered why it didn't do the same at this door as well. His curiosity is growing stronger, so he picks up a nearby rock and tosses it. The rock freezes mid-air as blue sparks scatter around it before fading quickly to reveal a gray frame around the rock, transforming it into a picture of its own. Now afraid, Carmen backs away, slamming the door shut, fearing his fate if he completely passes through the door as the rock had. Would he turn into a lifeless painting forever as well? He wonders why Domonic would create the door to this universe. What purpose would it serve?

He carefully looks through four more doors despite the adrenaline racing through his veins from fear as he faces the unknown dangers behind each door. The mysterious sparks and the knowledge of what lies within floods his brain at almost every door. How was this happening to him? No literature has described sparks while touching the doors or knowledge of the universes flooding to those as they entered. The universes remained a mystery after Domonic's death since all discovery attempts ceased when the dangers of the doors became more apparent. Creatures and armies would break through from time to time, torturing and killing innocent people. After countless battles and deaths, the three world leaders commanded the doors to be sealed shut to stop the bloodshed. Carmen wonders if the flood of knowledge is part of his unknown powers.

The whispering voice has yet to be found. He needs to check the seventh door, but this door is rumored to be the one that caused the horrific attack all those centuries ago. The door has vines growing all over it. Unlike the others, this one is locked with two-inch thick chains and a huge padlock. Carmen sighs as he hesitantly taps the lock. Unexpectedly, a small ball of orange light shoots from his finger, entering the lock's keyhole. There is a loud clicking sound as the lock falls from the chains and hits the ground. He carefully pulls the chains and vines off the door. Now visible, he can see the black door, with warnings carved all over it.

"KEEP OUT!"

"NEVER OPEN!"

"YOU WILL DIE!"

Carmen knows ignoring these warnings could endanger the entire kingdom. Still, the whispering sounds intensify, beckoning him to enter. Vibration radiates off the door in waves, hypnotizing him. He reaches for the doorknob mindlessly and continuously pulls as hard as possible; the door will not budge. He starts kicking at it to break it loose with no luck. With one final kick, Carmen knocks himself back, stumbling to the ground and knocking him out of the hypnotic haze. He stands up, brushing off dirt as he stares at the door, defeated, and begins to walk away. If the door is this stuck, it must be for a reason.

Almost back to his post, a loud scream echoes from behind him as a sudden gust of air slams into him, sending him face-first into the ground. Carmen rolls onto his back and looks towards the black door to see it creaking open ever so slightly. He stares in awe, wonder, and fear at what lies behind this door. Puzzled, he hurries to his feet and brushes his legs off. Slowly walking over to the door, Carmen pulls at the handle, and the door flings open quickly. Inside the door, a black and purple vortex with faint hues of other colors swirl around, leaving Carmen speechless.

This is the most beautiful thing Carmen has ever seen in his life. He gazes into the vortex, hypnotized by its striking colors and movements. He soon finds himself being pulled in, he tries pulling himself out, but it's too late. The vortex is forcefully sucking him in. His hands grip the edges of the door frame as he continues to try and pull himself out. With a slip of his fingers, he falls in spinning with the swirling colors. The door slams shut behind him, trapping him in this unknown universe. Carmen falls down a dark path of emptiness that feels like an eternity. The colors fade, leaving him in total darkness. He closes his eyes, hoping for it all to end or, better yet, a sign that this is all just a bad dream. Suddenly, he lands harshly on his back with a thud, knocking the wind out of him. He lays there for a few minutes in pain, moaning and groaning, trying to regain his breath. After a moment, he stands up and looks around this new world. All around him are giant leaves and trees, though he can't see what's in the distance due to the misty darkness of his new surroundings.

"Am I in a jungle? Where are the animals?" Carmen accidentally lets his terrified thoughts escape into the unknown. Looking up to the sky in despair, he notices the closed door floating in the sky. Maybe he can reach it and reopen the door.

Carmen takes a deep breath and clenches his fist, leaping forward. The earth under him breaks away like he pushed it away instead of jumping into the air. He smiles for a second; this is something he's never been able to do before. His proud moment is cut short when he remembers what needs to be done. He pushes forward to race up to the door as quickly as possible, hoping it will let him back in. Inches away, he reaches for the knob on the door. An orange spark shoots from his fingers connecting with the knob. As the spark encases the door, he watches it fade away like dust in the breeze.

He lets out a gasp as he loses his focus. The earth beneath his feet crumbles, knocking him out of the sky. He grips his hands together, trying to pull the earth together again to stop himself from smashing into the hard ground. This time, he's not as lucky with his control and can't pull the air and earth together to catch himself. Carmen hits the ground hard, smashing his head on a rock.

Struggling to find his balance, he makes it to his feet again. With blurred vision, he starts walking around to see if he can use anything to help himself. He wipes his hands over his face, trying to clear the blood from his eyes as it runs down his face from the wound on his forehead. His hands tremble as they brush over the large gash on his head. In a panic, seeing no other options, he screams out for help as loud as he can even with the searing pain in his head. All he hears in return are his own echoes.

He continues walking through the darkness, questioning if he will die alone. He bumps into the surrounding trees and trips over the rocks and roots beneath him. As Carmen gives up hope, he sees a flame in the distant trees. Not knowing who or what it could be, he starts racing through the jungle as fast as possible. Struggling to see and focus, he forgets about all the previous rocks and roots

he's tripped over until he falls, once again
hitting his head. His ears begin to ring as his
head sways from dizziness. He tries pushing
himself up again, but the strength in his arms
fade. He can see a fuzzy glow before him but
can't make anything out with his vision
blurring. He takes in one more deep breath
before laying his head on the ground, giving up
his fight. Slowly, he closes his eyes, letting
himself slip into unconsciousness on the cold,
wet ground.

The Girl With A Way

Carmen awakes in a dimly lit room on a thin bed. The bed creaks as he tries to take in his new surroundings, noticing a small floral dresser, basket with a blanket to his left and a desk at his feet. The desk has three neatly stacked books and a picture of a couple with a little girl sitting on the ground in front of a tree. The man looks to be in his mid-30s with light brown hair and a thick mustache. His bright green eyes stood out as if glowing. He towers over a woman standing next to him. The woman looks to be in her late thirties with long, flowing red hair and rosy cheeks. The little girl looks about eight, with red hair and round puffy cheeks. They are all dressed in brightly colored leather clothing. Above the desk is a small window with brown curtains that Carmen can see a tiny bit of light shining through.

"Is it morning time? How long have I been out? It doesn't quite look like sunlight outside,"

Carmen thinks out loud. Noticing a slight movement in the corner where the basket is, Carmen studies the basket with the blanket over it. The blanket is a blue and green color that appears to be knitted. As he stares intently at it, he notices the slight movement underneath the blanket. Again, Carmen studies it momentarily, contemplating what is hidden underneath, maybe a young pup? Carmen sits up slowly, the bed squeaks loudly under his weight. His head snaps to the door in a panic as he hears footsteps coming. He pulls the covers up, hiding half of his face with the thin blanket like a shield. A girl walks in, her long red hair glows against her pale skin, her bright green eyes twinkle in the glow of the candlelight that lights the room. She lets out a small giggle at Carmen's sad attempt to hide. He slowly lowers the blanket, his eyes fixate on her, hypnotized by her beauty. She stares back into his ocean-blue eyes for a moment before clearing her throat.

"How are you feeling? It seems you got into a nasty fight out there. You would have died if I hadn't found you." The girl says, her voice calm and smooth. She walks over to the dresser, her red hair swaying as she glides across the room. Carmen notices she is carrying a small silver platter with a white floral pot and matching cups. After setting the platter on the dresser, she carefully sits on the bed beside him. His eyes follow her movements as she reaches out towards his head. Carmen pulls back, wincing at the sharp pain her touch causes, not having noticed the injury on his head while he was distracted looking around the room. The girl doesn't pull back or hesitate; instead, she continues checking his wounds until she's satisfied. She smiles, pleased with her healing work. She sits back and raises an eyebrow at him as she waves her hand to prompt him to answer her question.

"I-I-I feel pretty good for the most part, just a little sore," Carmen says, still staring at the girl in awe. The girl giggles nervously, noticing the look on his face, and tilts her head, letting her hair fall like a curtain around her face to hide the blush blooming on her cheeks.

"Tea?" She lifts a hand, gesturing at the pot on the dresser. Carmen nods, turning his gaze from her for the first time since she entered the room.

"So, what were you doing in the woods? It's not a very safe place to be, especially at night; that's when the animals come out to hunt." The girl gets up from the bed and starts pouring the tea.

The blanket falls from his shoulders, Carmen tries to sit himself up in the bed. Scrapes and scratches cover his chest and stomach. He briefly studies the marks; they don't hurt and look like they are healing already. Carmen jumps, startled as the girl clears her throat. She has been standing there holding a cup of tea, waiting for him to gather his thoughts. Shaking his head as he realizes she has finished pouring the tea, he reaches for the cup; his finger grazes the side of her hand as he grabs the cup, and an orange spark jumps between them. The girl jumps back, almost spilling the tea. Carmen is unfazed as he is starting to welcome this bizarre occurrence. He doesn't see it as a threat but rather as a friendly guidance. He can't explain it, but it's almost as if it is trying to tell him what he needs to do, somehow showing him where to go and the path he needs to follow.

He begins to tell his story of how he ended up in the woods, He describes his duty of standing guard over the doors to different universes, and how he got sucked in following the unknown voice. The girl listens carefully as he explains, eager to learn more about her mysterious patient; she can't believe there are other universes besides hers. She has always loved exploring, but the island is all she has ever known. Anyone brave enough to venture off into the waters never got more than a couple hundred feet before they were struck down by mysterious storms. A million questions swirl in her mind, but she hesitates, not wanting to interrupt and risk losing out on any details. When Carmen finishes his story, they sit silently on the bed, letting the details sink in. Moments later, the girl's eyes widen, as she looks at Carmen with hopeful eyes full of excitement.

"I think I know a way we can get you home. A dragon on the far north side of the island can create portals to send you anywhere on the island. Maybe he can create one to get you home. He usually requires payment of some sort, but that depends on what he wants from whoever is requesting his services. He has a visionary that can see people's paths and usually wants something they will come across that interests him." Carmen sits up fast and looks at the girl with excitement.

"That's great!" Carmen pushes himself up further, trying to jump out of the bed.

"Calm down now. I don't know what he will ask for, but it's always something big, and it will take a few days to get there, but if we stick together, we can get you home. Tomorrow, I will *find my maps and plan our travel route."* The girl puts her hand on Carmen's shoulder and pushes him back on to bed. *"I want you to rest tonight. It will give the tea time to do its job. I added some Valetudo berries, which help speed up healing from days to hours."* She pushes the cup in his hands closer to his face. He doesn't hesitate and just takes a big gulp. He feels no reason not to trust her. Although he forgot to ask her name, he feels safe around her. His eyes widen briefly as he realizes he has forgotten to ask her name!

"Oh my, where are my manors? My name is Carmen Animus, prince of Animus Kingdom. And who might you be, my lady?" he asks in an awkward half-bow while sitting upright in bed. The girl giggles slightly at Carmen's attempt at a polite bow.

"Oh my, I am sorry, my name is Julia Silva, lady of this, uh cabin... I guess... It's such a pleasure being in the presence of royalty." She jumps off the edge of the bed to give Carmen her best curtsy. Her ankle rolls slightly; she stumbles back, catching herself on the end of

the bedpost. The two burst into laughter as Julia sits quickly on the end of the bed, trying not to embarrass herself more.

"That's such a pretty name," Carmen says with a slight wink as he sips the rest of his tea. He leans slightly over the bed to rest the empty cup on the dresser beside him. "So we have to wait until tomorrow to leave? Are you sure you can assist me on the journey to the Dragon King? You know, being the lady of the cabin and all, you must be pretty busy." He turns more to reach the dresser to pour himself another cup of tea. Julia holds her hand and motions for him to settle down as she gets up from the bed. He watches her pour a new cup of tea as he settles back into bed; she is slow and graceful, giving off a completely calm and relaxed aura.

"You're not well enough with that nasty cut on your head. I want you to rest for now, and yes, I'm going with you. You don't want to go alone; it's not safe; I know the island's dangers like the back of my hand. Trust me, you're gonna need me. I don't get out often other than hunting and foraging. This will give me new excitement in my life." She gives Carmen a stern look as if to say, get your rest or else. Carmen smiles at her fierce courage and independence as she hands him the cup and turns to walk out of the room.

As Julia's figure disappears around the corner of the short hallway outside the room, Carmen notices the movement in the basket again from the edge of his vision. He looks to the side to see that the blanket covering the basket is still moving up and down steadily like something is breathing. He gets out of bed, carefully walks over to the basket, and slowly grabs the edge of the blanket with a shaking hand. Quickly ripping off the blanket, he lets out a high-pitched yell at what lies underneath. A light gray baby dragon with black dots down his furry back sits inside the basket. Julia comes running into the room to see the problem. She giggles hysterically, slapping her knee at the sight of Carmen and the baby dragon.

"It's not funny, don't laugh at me. Isn't it dangerous? Why does it have fur everywhere? Where are its scales? DON'T DRAGONS HAVE SCALES? " Carmen yells in an agitated voice. Julia continues laughing, ignoring the nasty look he's giving her.

"I'm sorry for laughing, but he's only a baby. Baby dragons have fur, not scales. He will get his scales in a few days. Dragons are notoriously fast growers" Julia stops laughing, picks up the baby dragon, and shows it to Carmen. "He is only a baby, so he doesn't know the cruelty that the other dragons know. I hope that if I raise him with love, he will grow up to be kind and gentle. Carmen's anger subsides upon hearing her intentions. He places his hand on the dragon's belly and rubs his hand back and forth, surprised at how extremely soft and smooth the fur is. The baby dragon lets out a little squeak as it stretches its long neck to rub its head against Carmen's arm. He takes the baby in his hands and holds him gently, rocking back and forth in his arms while patting his belly. *"Do you not have dragons where you're from?"* Julia asks as he cradles the dragon.

"No, they're just myths in stories that our elders tell. There is a book I once read about a dragon attack long ago, but no one has seen one since. Does he have a name?" Carmen asks in a sweet, calming voice. She looks at him with gentle eyes as he holds the baby with such care. His nurturing gesture makes Julia's heart flutter.

"Yes, I have named him Cypress," She replies, taking the baby dragon from Carmen's arms and placing him carefully back into the basket. "He also should still be sleeping," she mumbles mockingly. She boops his nose with hers and pulls the blanket back over him. She pats the lump under the blanket, tucking the edges of the blanket into the basket around the lump, and starts walking back toward the door.

"Baby dragons should get several hours of sleep daily."

"How did you acquire a baby dragon?" Carmen asks as he gently slips into the bed, trying not to make another loud squeak. Julia turns and looks at Carmen with a blank expression. Her eyes sad and filled with hurt.

"I found his mother dead in the woods. She had been killed by hunters. I was going to leave before they got to her when I realized she had an egg clutched in her chest cavity. Something in me told me to take the egg. I managed to get away before the hunters found the body. I kept him warm until he hatched. I got books on dragons from the library to learn how to care for them. Unfortunately, most of them are on how to kill dragons." Julia's head drops as she leans against the door frame.

"That was very kind and noble. Cypress is lucky to have you when his mother was taken too soon." He stares at the lump caringly. This was a whole new world with a lot for him to learn. All he had known about dragons were the stories of the violent attacks that came from

the doors before they were locked up. He needs
to explore this world with an open mind. Things
may not be as bad as he or the others have
heard.

"Thank you," she says, blushing as she
leaves the room. Carmen watches her backside
again as she leaves with more awe of her
beauty in his eyes. As Carmen waits for Julia to
return, he wonders what everyone in the
kingdom would think or do when they realize
his absence. This would surely anger his father;
he knows better than to touch the doors. Let
alone open them. How would he explain what
he's seen or experienced without telling them
he unlocked the forbidden doors? Carmen's
fears change as he wonders where Julia's
parents are. She is much too young to be living
alone. She seems well off, but it is still strange
to him. Being such a beautiful girl, how can she
not have a boyfriend? Carmen changes his
puzzled expression when he hears Julia's
footsteps approaching him. She enters the
room with another silver tray. This one

contains fresh wraps for Carmen's head. A small wooden cup, sponges, and a small set of metal pinchers are next to the wraps.

"Please drink some more tea. I need you to finish the pot to get the full effect of the berries," Julia remarks as she rechecks the cut on his head. Carmen winces every time she pokes at his wound. He feels her tugging and pulling his hair as she inspects the healing. Carefully, she picks up the sponge and dips it in the cup. She brushes aside his black hair before dabbing it on his wound; Carmen pulls back, shouting, *"OUCH."* Julia places her hand under his chin and pulls his head back. Carmen grits his teeth, bearing the pain until Julia puts the blood-soaked sponge back on the silver tray. She carefully wraps the bandages around Carmen's head, re-covering the wound. Carmen's head spins as he stares at the bloody sponge. He reaches up to pat the bandages as Julia slaps his hand down. *"The bleeding has stopped. I'm just trying to clean off the dried blood to keep it clean while the tea heals you. We should be able to remove the bandages by*

morning." Julia picks up the tray to move it out of Carmen's sight. She doesn't want him to panic. Carmen nods as he looks back at the photo on the desk.

"Are those your parents? Where are they? If you don't mind me asking, you don't seem old enough to live alone out here." Carmen questions in an inquisitive voice. Julia hands him a fresh cup of tea as she sighs. Carmen can see her eyes welling with sadness. She sits on the edge of the bed, pulling her legs up to cross them under her.

"Well, they were killed. I'm unsure exactly what happened to them; everyone tells me different stories, and I don't know whom to believe. But I believe my grandmother did it," she confesses, still looking at the floor.

"I was only seven years old when she came home and woke me up and told me my parents had died in a horrible accident. She said a dragon had killed them when they were trying to get berries to make a cake for my birthday. I started to cry. But she didn't; she had an eerie smile and seemed unfazed. I can still see the

look on her face every time I think about them. She said she had to leave to go get supplies for us. We were going to live together, but she never came back. I've lived here on my own ever since. It was hard for a while cause I was so young and had no idea what I was doing, but I have met a lot of sweet people who have helped me along the way." A small tear rolls from the corner of Julia's eye.

"I am so sorry. I can't imagine how hard it must have been for you. How does that make your grandma the murderer?" Carmen leans forward, wiping the tear from her cheek. She looks up at him, their eyes meet. He pulls back quickly, afraid he's overstepping.

"The king's army found her horse next to their bodies; it had blood all over its feet. My grandmother was nowhere to be found. She always fought with my father and hated him for some reason unknown to me." Julia looks up at Carmen.

"Oh my lord, I'm sorry for your loss, and I'm sorry I brought it up in the first place. I can tell that it's a touchy subject for you. I can't imagine how hurt you feel. My mother passed giving birth to me so I never got the chance to meet her." Carmen expressed sadly, taking Julia's hand in his.

"No, it's okay. It's good to talk about things like that to let our anger out," Julia proclaims with a brighter look in her eyes. "So now that I shared, do you know what caused your mother to pass?" Julia asks as she looks deep into Carmen's eyes.

"Well, after I was born, she was bleeding a lot. Our best healers didn't know what to do. My father told me she was in a lot of pain, got really sick within minutes, and before he knew it, she was gone. I had never met her, but I felt like I knew her. My father talks about her all the time. He tells me all the great things she did for the kingdom and surrounding villages." Julia has a slight twinkle in her eyes as she leans in to hug Carmen. Carmen sits there awkwardly before pushing his arms around her. The two embrace for what seems like hours. Each of them lets out a small sigh of relief. Julia lets go of Carmen and gets off the bed. She walks over to the door.

"Well, now that we have shared and found something in common, I think you should finish your tea and get some rest. If you want to get home, I need to head out to get some supplies for our trip." She gives Carmen a smile, her eyes gleaming as she looks at him momentarily before walking out the door. She pulls the door shut behind her with a loud creek. Carmen can hear little squeaks and squeals from Cypress. The sound of the door causes him to stir, but luckily he hasn't woken up. Lucky him for being such a heavy sleeper, Carmen thinks to himself as he rolls his eyes wishing the same for himself.

Carmen sits silently on the bed for a moment to finish his tea. When he finishes, he gets out of bed, walks to the dresser, and places the cup on the tray. It feels nice to be on his feet again, finally. He stretches for a moment before getting back into bed. As caring and sweet as Julia is, he doesn't want to upset her by disobeying her orders to rest. He has a feeling he is going to need his full strength for their coming adventure. Carmen nestles himself into the bed to set off to sleep—his mind races. So much has happened quickly, causing many questions to spiral through his head.

Grandma, Is That You?

Carmen awakes the following day, his nose twitching. Julia must be cooking. He smells the sweetest of aromas. Carmen pushes the blankets off his legs and rolls out of bed. He quietly tiptoes over to where Cypress is sleeping and rubs the still-motionless lump. He notices Julia had been in the room at some point; the tray and books are missing from the dresser. Carmen stands in the middle of the room for a few moments. He places his hand on his head and realizes the bandages had been removed while he was asleep. The tea worked! No cuts or scraps, not even a sign of blood; it had healed him overnight. Amazed, he walks out of the room and enters a long, dark hallway to find Julia. The walls are blank, with raw wood planks, and the floor is a green mossy-like carpeting. The hall leads to a small kitchen with a table in the center. The walls are made of the same wood as the hall, and everything is unpainted. Julia sits at the table with her maps and journals on one side and large plates full of food and juice on the other. It reminds Carmen of how his dad used to make breakfast every Sunday until the duties of the Kingdom became too much. He pulls out a chair across from her; he watches her shuffle through the papers and put marks all over the map.

"Good morning; how are you feeling? Have something to eat; I made plenty to share," Julia says, not looking up from her work. Carmen's stomach lets out a loud gurgling noise. It has been some time since he's eaten, and with a nod, he begins to dig in.

"I feel incredible! That tea worked wonders. Let's not forget your amazing nursing skills." Carmen winks. Julia lets a slight giggle slip through her lips. Her cheeks grow rosie red. She pulls the book to her face to cover her blushing between bites. Carmen notices her hiding. He can feel the warmth rising in his own face. He hangs his head low towards his plate and continues eating to hide his blushing.

"Well, whatever it was, I am glad you're feeling better. I am almost done planning our trip. We should be there in only one week's time. It will be hard, and there are some dangerous places we will have to travel through, but I think I have us on the best route to get there safely. We can head out when we're done eating; I've packed all we need. If we run out of water, the stream will not be too far from the trail I have set. It's only half a mile at most from the trail." Julia starts showing Carmen the map, and he looks at it intently. Although he had no knowledge of the land and its dangers, it is still a mystery to him how the other doors gave him knowledge. Still, this one gives him nothing, leaving him completely lost without Julia's help. While the two eat together, Julia points out all the landmarks on the map and the different areas they will venture through. She even marked where they would need to sleep or rest to maintain energy and daylight. As they finish eating, Julia clears the remaining food, packing it in paper bags lined with a strange glaze so they can eat later when they get hungry. Carmen takes the dirty dishes and brings them to the large washing basin on the other side of the kitchen. Puzzled, he places the dishes in the basin to wash them. This is different from the one in his castle. There is no hand pump for running water. Julia whistles as she points out the window at a well with a bucket hanging from the spigot. Carmen sighs loudly, realizing he has been spoiled by the luxury of water pumping directly to the basin.

"Sorry, Your Majesty, I don't have a maid to help you." Julia mockingly winks at him as he rolls his eyes with a slight chuckle. He cautiously ventures outside to grab some water. It's warm with a cool breeze out. The tree tops are thick, but sunlight still manages to break through. The outside of the house looks like a pile of logs placed together to form a home. The ground is covered in thick moss that is soft on his feet. Birds chirp somewhere in the trees. The smell of the forest invites him to explore;

he even smells the remains of the fire where breakfast was cooked. Next to the well is a large fire pit lined with stones still smoldering with embers. There's a sizable flat stone leaning against the wall of the pit. Julia must have used this stone as a cooktop; it looks scorched on one side. He's only seen steel plates or grates be used. Carmen realizes he has been distracted by his thoughts, so he lowers the bucket into the well. He looks down to see the bottom, but it's too deep. All he can see is pure darkness. He sits back quickly and lowers the bucket faster. He fills three buckets before the basin is full enough to wash all the dirty dishes. Julia giggles as she watches him. She can tell he's not accustomed to such manual labor. Things at the castle are probably done for him by others.

"Before we go, we need to get you some fresh clothing. I pulled out some of my dad's clothing. You're about the same build, so they should fit." She hands him the bundle of neatly folded clothes. Carmen brushes the top of Julia's hand as he grabs the clothes. She pulls back as another orange spark jumps between them, catching her eyes. Carmen walks into the bedroom and pulls off his pants; he hears a tiny squeak from behind him. He spins around to see Cypress awake, covering his eyes. He takes the knitted blanket and puts it over Cypress' head; he continues changing as he chuckles. Julia was right; the clothing fits almost perfectly. The pants and shirt are brown with tan stripes on the arms and legs. The vest is thick leather with a hard, mossy green dyed wax coating. The buckles to the pants and vest are gold-plated and carved with a vine-like design. The whole design looks warrior-esk. Even the boots match the outfit, brown and mossy green with red laces and gold-plated thread holes and aglets. After examining his new style, Carmen walks to Cypress picking him up from the basket. He cradles him in his arms like a baby, rubbing his belly as they greet Julia in the kitchen. She smiles at the two for a moment as she brushes by, making her way to the bedroom to change. Carmen plays with Cypress as they wait. He feels a strange attachment to Cypress. The orange sparks dance around as he pats his fuzzy friend's belly, which gives him comfort and security. Cypress doesn't seem to mind the sparks as he wiggles and squeals excitedly. Carmen is sure something is telling him this is where he needs to be. When Julia comes out of the room, Carmen's mouth drops. Julia's now wearing short, tight brown shorts with a blue and gold dagger fastened to the outside of her thigh. Her shirt which barely reaches the top of her belly button is brown with tan swirls and green stripes down the side. She also has a red bandana wrapped around her left arm with another dagger. On her back is a bow with a quiver containing a single arrow.

"Are you just going to stare at me, or are we going to head out?" Julia asks sarcastically, giggling as his face grows red with embarrassment. She walks to the door and grabs a large green backpack off the end table next to the door. Carmen shakes his head in embarrassment when he realizes he has been gawking at her. He quickly follows behind, grabbing another large tan bag from the floor by the end table. As they approach the door, Julia stops. "Wait, I forgot something." She turns around and rushes to her room. Once inside, she walks over to the dresser, grabs the picture of her parents, and puts it into her bag.

Outside, Carmen tosses Cypress in the air as he squeals and flaps his little wings, pretending to fly. Julia clears her throat as she pulls the green bag from her back and takes out a bundle of cloth. She extends it to Carmen, who is staring at her, confused.

"This was my father's. He told me it would be mine one day and serve me well. As you can see, I am a bow kind of girl, like my mum, so I have no need for this." Carmen grabs the bundle from her hands and begins to unravel it. Inside the cloth is what looks like the handle of a sword. The handle is heavy, solid silver with golden lines looping around it like ripples in water. He turns it over, wondering where the rest of it is. Is this some kind of joke? He brushes his hand over the handle, feeling its smooth edges. The orange spark from his hands connects with it. "You need to use energy magic to reveal the sword. Those who are worthy can make the blade appear. Something deep in my heart tells me I was destined to give this to you." Julia takes the handle from Carmen to show him how to fasten it to his belt. "I keep noticing those orange sparks from your hands. I know you're still trying to figure out what they mean, but I think you should listen to them. They seem like they are guiding you." Julia gives Carmen a wink before turning to readjust her bag onto her back.

"Thank you. This is the most thoughtful gesture, but this can't be meant for me. I can barely control my powers, let alone be worthy enough to use this sword." Carmen drops his right hand to his side, feeling the handle on his hip. He feels energy radiating off it, almost like it's alive. It feels like it's trying to communicate something to him. Carmen's uncle Menius had taught Carmen that in order for him to better control his powers. He must feel the energy around him, listen to them, trust them, and they will guide you. "You don't even know me. Why would you give up something so special from your father, no less."

"I've been alone long enough to know when to trust my gut. My father always told me to follow my heart. I know in my heart this is the right thing to do." Carmen looks up, stunned. Julia's eyes are twinkling in the sunlight. He smiles as he nods in thanks.

"Do we need to find you more arrows? It seems you're missing a few." Carmen questions. Julia steps back, pulling the bow and arrow out of her quiver, and holds it out to Carmen. She quickly draws back, pointing it right at his face. His eyes grow wide with fear as he sinks back. She giggles at his sudden terror.

Julia spins fast, with the smoothest motion Carmen has ever seen. She releases the draw, shooting the arrow into the woods at a tree. With an explosion, the arrow pierces through the tree and turns around, flying back at Carmen and Julia. Carmen falls to the ground, covering his head. Julia giggles, unmoved, as the arrow stops just before her and hovers in place. She grabs the arrow and places it back in the quiver. Carmen looks up unamused.

"She won't harm you unless I want her to. She can see what I desire her to do." She reaches down to grab Carmen's hand to help him get off the ground. He lets out a nervous chuckle as he dusts himself off. "Just know you piss me off, and you'll be sure to find this arrow shoved somewhere you don't want it." Carmen gulps as he shakes his head with understanding. Julia laughs as she pets his shoulder. "This arrow is forged from the strongest, lightest materials on the island. Practically indestructible and ruthless yet delicate and loyal. Once paired with a soul, this arrow will return to its master. It was my mother's, and when she passed, I was picked as her new partner, and she has served me well. This is the only arrow I will ever need."

"Your parents would be so proud of you. Smart, strong, and powerful, I presume." Julia chuckles at the thought.

"No, no, no. I have no powers. I am just a regular person." Carmen tilts his head with confusion; where he came from, everyone has powers. Not everyone learns how to use them or wants to, but they still have them. Julia shrugs; she doesn't seem worried; she has held her own all this time without powers. They continue talking as they set off into the woods. Cypress follows, his little legs moving quickly, causing a playful bouncing run to help him keep up. He squeals each time he finds a pinecone he can crunch with his foot. Julia and Carmen laugh at him as they find pinecones to crush with him.

After a while, walking with Cypress starts taking its toll on Carmen and Julia. They need to stop frequently to let him rest; they even take turns holding him as he sleeps. Eventually, Carmen moves the items around between the bags to empty one of them out so they can use it as a carrier. Cypress nestles into the bag and falls fast asleep. Although easier to carry, he isn't light enough to carry for long periods. Even Julia is struggling with all the extra items now in her bag. The two push through for another few miles before they arrive at a large cave and decide to stop for the night. Despite the few setbacks with Cypress, they still make it a good 15 miles. Julia holds her hands to the sky to measure the sun's distance, but it is still a couple of hours before sunset. Julia and Carmen agree it will be best to take their time and not over-exert their energy.

"This is Witches Den Cave. Years ago, covens would meet here to perform rituals and ceremonies. It hasn't been used in years since the covens moved north to the valleys." Julia pulls out the map to show Carmen where they are. This is the first time she has pulled out the map, as she knows the land like the back of her hand and can navigate it with her eyes closed. They cautiously walk into the cave in case another passerby or animal has taken refuge. The narrow and tight opening opens up to a large canal that goes for miles. The air is musty and warm; water drips can be heard echoing down the long stretch. The cave walls are covered in drawings of runes and other unknown writing. Claw marks and candle wax are smeared on the walls and ground from previous rituals. They continue walking further into the cave. They come to an opening off to the side of the hall. There's light coming from the room. The two walk-in slowly; Julia grips her bow. The room is large and well-lit, with torches lining the walls. An old lady is in the back, rocking in a rocking chair. She is dressed in a long, thick black robe with a hood over her head covering part of her face. As they get closer, Julia squints, trying to get a better look as her hands grip the bow tighter.

"Grandma, is that you?" Julia stops walking as she grabs Carmen's sleeve to pull him back. With an evil laugh, the old woman stands up. A large smile stretches across her face as she pulls her hood back. Her white hair falls from the hood to the front of her shoulders. She goes to take a step forward

when Julia seizes her arrow and pulls back on the bow.

"Well, well, it's been such a long time. I've been waiting for this moment, and now it's finally here!" The witch takes a step, and Julia stomps her foot to say stop. The witch laughs and draws back slightly. Her crooked smile looks Julia up and down.

"What are you talking about?" Julia demands angrily. "I know you killed my parents; I want the truth." Julia's eyes flare at the old woman. Carmen stands watching as the two have their stare down.

"My, how you have grown, my darling. You look just like your mother. She was always the one with all the looks. She could have had anyone she wanted, and she chose your disgusting father." The witch rolls her eyes and snarls at the idea. Shaking her head she snaps back with her crooked smile. "Don't tell me you haven't figured it out yet! You had ten years. Yes, I did it. But do you know why I had to do *it?"* The witch laughs again. This infuriates Julia.

"Because you hate the fact my mother married my father, a knight. It's like you didn't want the best for her or her happiness," screamed Julia.

"Good guess, but no, you have something I want, and your mother was stupid to have given it to you. I tried taking it back that night, but it almost killed me, so I had to leave." The witch stretches out her long, stick-like arm and points her long, crooked finger at Julia. She lets go of the bowstring, hurtling the arrow at her grandmother. With a twitch of her finger, the arrow stops dead, dropping to the ground. Carmen lunges forward with a hand on the sword handle. Julia holds out her arm, pushing him back.

"MY ARROW! HOW DID YOU DO THAT!" Julia pulls back, a little frightened and puzzled. She gestures her head, and the arrow retreats back to her. *"I don't have anything of yours."* Julia stands her ground, trying to push back her

feelings. That arrow is meant to always protect her.

"The rest of our powers, you got them before your stupid bitch of a mother died. She gave them to you when she decided to leave the coven, which was a big mistake but fixable. You see, your mother had her choice. She broke the rules of the coven by marrying a mortal, but we were willing to overlook that and let her leave willingly. All she had to do was surrender her powers back to the coven. Instead, she gave them to you. I was tasked with taking care of her and collecting what belonged to the coven. I gave her the option to just give me her power, and I would leave her be and tell the coven she was dead, but she chose to fight back. She had already given all the magic she had to you. So she was weak and died with the snap of my fingers. It was not my proudest moment, but she made her choice. As for your father, well, he was in the wrong place at the wrong time, so I couldn't leave any witnesses. Your precious arrow and that sword on his hip were also ours. They were created by the coven to protect us. They've been enchanted not to harm anyone of the coven." The witch holds her hand up, now keeping an eye on Carmen. Julia's anger softens as she runs through the emotions in her head. She has no idea what to believe or what is true anymore. Could her mom really have betrayed the coven so poorly? If she had, why? There had to be a reason her mother wouldn't just take something that wasn't hers, would she?

"I don't understand why she would give them to me. Why couldn't you just take them back and leave me be like you did all those years ago?" Carmen grabs her arm as tears begin flowing down her face. The witch laughs and shoots a bolt of power at them, sending them flying. They smash into the cave walls. Cypress falls from Carmen's bag; now exposed to the witch, he lets out a loud whimper and runs out of the cave. The witch gives an evil laugh. Carmen jumps up and tries to help Julia get to her feet. Julia's legs buckle in pain.

"Your dad found out who we were when you were seven. He got angry and told your mom to stay away from us. She informed us she would be parting ways, and obviously, we weren't happy, but we gave her her options. We *have no idea why she did what she did, knowing very well the consequences that would ensue. After they were taken care of, I tried to take them back, but before your mother died, she placed a curse on you so we couldn't touch you. I've been watching you for years. I knew her curse would weaken over time and she wouldn't be able to recast the spell. It was only a matter of time before it wore off, and I would be able to take them back. It just worked out perfectly that you found me here first."* Julia sobs harder. Carmen struggles to get Julia off the ground, her legs still shaking.

"How could you? You're my Grandmother." Julia squeezes Carmen's arm tight and pulls herself to her feet.

"Fool, I'm not your grandmother. That is the only way I knew how to get close to your family to get my powers, but you see how well that worked out for me. Myles came along and ruined everything," the witch says in a stern, annoyed voice.

"Oh my god, Myles, I forgot all about him. He was at the house when you left. He helped put me to bed. He would visit the house from

time to time to check on me. He just disappeared after a while. I haven't seen him in years." Julia speaks softly, with more tears starting to well up in her eyes.

"Well, that's because I killed him too. Now it's time, Julia, give me your powers." The witch commands as she raises her hand, pointing at Julia. *"If you don't give them to me now, I'll take them by force, and you will suffer the same fate as your mother and father."* The evil witch laughs as she raises her hand and points at Carmen and Julia. A green bolt shoots from her finger, striking Julia. She screams out in pain as a green aura consumes her being. Carmen can see the power draining from her. This is nothing like he's seen before; no one possesses this power. There was no such thing as power transfer in his universe. Carmen instinctively reaches out and touches the green bolt connecting the two together. The bolt turns red, reaching back to the witch, and Julia's aura turns purple. Orange sparks consume him, and his face goes blank. He has no idea what is happening but has no control over himself. He

flicks his wrist, and the witch flies into the wall. Raising his arm, he pulls down hard. The cave shakes violently as rocks come loose and tumble down on the witch. He grabs Julia's hand and, with a newfound strength, lifts her off the ground into his arms and runs out of the cave. He dodges falling rocks as he runs to the opening of the cave. He pushes off with his feet, sending him and Julia flying. The opening to the cave rumbles shut as it caves in. Dust and dirt fill the air around them. He hovers his body over Julia as he holds her in his arms. His orange glow begins to fade and gives him back his control.

"Julia, are you okay?" Carmen asks, cradling Julia in his arms. The two of them cough, clearing their throats from dust and dirt.

"Yes, I'm fine. Thank you for saving me. How did you do that? Do you think she's dead?" Julia wipes the tears from her face with wide eyes. She's grateful he's here, but her mind races with everything that has come to light. She has powers she doesn't know how to use, and everything she knows is a lie.

"You are more than welcome! To be honest, I have no idea how I did that! Those are not powers people in my universe use or know of. I don't think anyone could have survived that. So much for being a regular human, huh?" Carmen gently smiles at her, lightening the mood. She smiles back, shaking her head. "I'll help you find out how to use them; we will learn together because I don't even know all of my own powers." Carmen and Julia look at each other for a moment. Julia studies his face as she feels a strange connection with him.

"You will?" Julia says, trying to break the silence. She has hope in her voice. She's been alone for so long and has no idea what to do for the first time in a long time. It will be nice to have someone around, to not be alone.

"Yes, you're my friend, you're helping me get home. It will be nice to return the favor and help you with something." Julia smiles big, putting her arms around Carmen's neck, and gives him a big hug and kisses him on the cheek. Carmen's face turns red, and Julia bows her head giggling. At the sound of Julia's giggle, Cypress comes flying over the top of the high cave. He lets out a loud squeak as if to say look at me! Julia's face lights up.

"OH MY, LOOK, HE'S FLYING!" Julia squeals, jumping from Carmen's arms in excitement. Carmen stands and watches in amazement. Cypress starts coming down to greet them. His left-wing freezes, and he falls from the sky. Carmen runs over to catch him. The two fumble around a bit as Cypress continues to try to flap his little wings to catch himself. He will need to build up strength in his wings. They stand there for a moment, patting Cypress and cuddling him. Their attention is caught by the sounds of more rocks tumbling as more of the cave collapses. Julia turns her attention to the map. She has to plan a route around the cave quickly.

"We shouldn't stay here. This cave is going to keep collapsing. We don't want to be caught

in a landslide or something." Carmen agrees and points to the map. He spots a route two miles back that will take them around the mountain.

A Night of Rest

F inally at a good place to rest, Carmen strings up a blanket for cover and makes their beds. After that he gathers some wood to build a fire. He places the wood in a triangle shape and waves his hands over it. With a harsh exhale a small fireball shoots from his hands lighting the wood. He looks at his hand. The power feels stronger and more controlled for the first time in his life. He has always struggled with his powers, but somehow being here they just come naturally to him without explanation. As he looks around, he wonders if the energy of this universe is causing his powers to flourish. Julia catches his eyes as she places the bundle of wood by the fire. Or is it this mysterious girl who saved his life? Is she somehow making him stronger? She has been a distraction to him since they met, but the closer she is to him, the stronger he feels.

He watches Julia venture away from their camp to set traps to try and catch a few rabbits they had seen hopping around. Carmen has only been hunting a few times. It is tradition for men to hunt; however, he has never successfully caught anything as it is viewed as a sport rather than a need. Since she grew up fending for herself, Julia is excited to hunt and food prep. Although visibly tired, Cypress happily stomps on pine cones, listening to them crunch. Like other babies, Cypress has that child-like mentality of wanting to do anything except what he needs to do. Right now, Cypress needs sleep.

After setting a few traps Julia sits by the fire resting against a tree stump. She grabs her bag pulling out three small bowls, two spoons, and a slightly larger bowl with a lid. It is filled with soup. Carmen raises an eyebrow surprised it hadn't popped open during the chaos. She places the bowl on two sticks balancing over the fire. She then pulls an apple from her bag and the small dagger from her arm, This piques

Cypress's interest, and he starts bouncing around squealing as Julia cuts a quarter chunk of apple and tosses it into the air. Cypress, with a push of his legs and a flap of his little wings, springs up into the air to catch the apple chunk. He perches himself on a branch high in the trees to munch on the apple in his little front paws.

"Now that you can fly it seems I'll have to get more clever with teaching you new tricks." Julia and Carmen laugh as they lean back to watch the fire. Julia rests her head on Carmen's shoulder and lets out a slight sigh. "Today has been exhausting, but I'm glad we make such a good team." Julia rolls her head slightly to look up at Carmen. She can see a smile on his face. She studies his face for a moment; even with the fire coloring everything a reddish-orange, she can see the blue in his eyes. Looking at Carmen, she realizes how safe she feels with him. She has never needed anyone to feel safe with. She has been alone for so long. But being beside him allows her to relax and let someone else be her strength. It feels nice.

"So, what's the plan for tomorrow?" Carmen asks with a huge yawn. Julia shakes her head, breaking her gaze on Carmen's eyes. She scrambles for her bag to retrieve the map. Carmen gets up to pull the bowl of soup from the fire. It has been there for quite some time. He spoons a small amount into each bowl and hands one of them to Julia.

"Where we had to change courses we will have to pass through dragon forest. We won't want to pass through until around noon. So that means we don't have to get up super early. Dragons are typically night hunters and sleep during the day. We will need to be quiet. Waking a sleeping dragon is the last thing you want to do, especially on their land." Julia giggles, watching Carmen wrinkle his nose as he yawns.

"Are dragons not typically friendly?" Carmen looks up at Cypress, who's still playing in the tree, hopping from branch to branch. Aside from Cypress, he has never met a dragon before and knows nothing about them.

"That's a bit of a loaded question," Julia says with a slight smile. "If you leave them alone, don't attack them or disturb their nest; they won't bother you. They don't take it kindly if you pass through dragon forest like we are. That area was given to them as a peace offering. They will hunt us on their land as we hunt them on ours. Before you ask, no, we can't go around. The royal dragons are another story. They can not kill anyone; however, they have nasty attitudes because they are used for their abilities, which are unlike other dragons. Some of the tasks they put people through can get them killed." Carmen's eyes are wide as she speaks. It seems everything here can and will kill you given the opportunity. Julia slurps her soup unfazed by the danger.

"Well I'm glad I have you on my team; I'd be dead otherwise."

Julia giggles while giving Carmen a smile and a slight shrug. The two of them sit there in silence as they finish their bowls of soup.

Cypress finally jumps down from the trees, crawling into Carmen's empty bag to sleep. After eating Carmen rinses the dishes in the nearby stream as Julia spreads out the coals of the fire. She wants to maintain the heat but dims out the light so they can sleep better. Carmen and Julia sleep side by side under the makeshift tent with Cypress between them.

That night, Carmen finds it hard to sleep. His mind twist with questions and worries. What will happen to him? What will his father do to him or think of him? How will the villagers respond to his mistake? With the door now unattended, everyone is at risk. Will he be welcomed back after breaking the rules? What if another guard locked it making their rounds and he can't get out? Carmen's thoughts slowly drift as he envisions Julia and Cypress returning with him. Julia has struggled enough in her life and just dropped everything to help him, a total stranger. Someone she had no reason to trust but gave all her trust and gentle kindness to. This gives him a warm feeling. Is this true love or is this just the idea of growing his family? He has always wanted something more than just him, his father, and his uncle. He never had a mother and the maids certainly never paid any mind to him even when he showed them the utmost kindness; he had always wondered what it would be like to have a big family. A dragon would be a hard concept for people to get used to but Cypress would win them over, he knows in his soul everyone would grow to love him. Carmen slowly drifts off as his mind creates wonderful images of family.

Dragon Forest

W hen Carmen awakes the following day, he rolls to his side, letting out a big yawn while stretching. Slowly letting out of the stretch, he rests his hand on where Cypress had been lying the night before. He jolts up when his hand hits the ground. Julia and Cypress are missing. Quickly, he scans his surroundings. Moving his hands to his mouth, he calls out their name. He listens briefly for a response. Hearing nothing but the sound of birds chirping, he looks over to the fire, even the blanket Carmen had set up as a canopy is gone.

All the supplies are gone.

Did they leave him to travel on his own?

Has Julia changed her mind about helping?

Carmen shakes his head to rid himself of the terrible thoughts. Julia wouldn't do that, she's too kind and caring. Taking a deep breath Carmen decides to head towards the river for a splash of water. As he approaches the water, he hears a familiar giggle and squealing. A big smile crosses his face as he picks up his pace, running towards the river. There they are, just splashing around in the water. Julia is scooping up handfuls of water and throwing them up in the air as Cypress flies back and forth through it. Julia catches Carmen watching them; she turns and waves him over.

"There you are! I have been searching everywhere for you two." Carmen says as he sits on a big rock near the river's edge. Julia lets out a giggle before dunking her head under the water. She comes up, smoothing her hair out of her face and waving Carmen into the water.

"Come on, get in; the water is so nice. I came out here to wash up and found a deep spot perfect for a little swim." Julia lays back in the water, letting her feet kick up and float on her back. Her long red hair floats over her head, swirling with the water. His face turns red, and he quickly averts his eyes up and behind him. He hadn't realized Julia was naked. "Are you shy or something?" Julia stops floating to stand up. She pulls her hair in front of her and turns around, covering her eyes. *"I'll even look away while you get in if that makes you feel better."* Julia giggles mockingly as she slowly turns around, peeking at him through her fingers. Hesitantly, Carmen sinks behind a large tree. Quickly, he takes off his clothes and jumps into the water, splashing Julia. Cypress flies over them, letting out squeals as he catches the water in the air.

"I'm not shy; I was caught off guard, that's all. I was raised to be a gentleman and never gawk at beautiful women." Julia raises an eyebrow, shaking her head at him, and calls him a liar. Carmen shrugs as he sinks into the water to dunk his head. The water is absolutely lovely. It's not super cold like other rivers. *"This*

gives me an idea!" Carmen yells out as he dives under the water and comes up with a rock smaller than his palm. Julia looks at him, confused. He levitates the rock and whips it at a nearby tree. Cypress takes off chasing the rock.

"Your grandma or witch whatever she is said you have powers; let's try and see what they are, right? Where I come from, water is one of the easiest to learn." Julia smiles big and nods excitedly. Carmen holds his hand with the rock on top. He lowers his hand so that only the back of his hand touches the water. *"Put your hands flat on the water, but don't submerge them. Think of the water as a living being and try to feel its vibrations, not just its movements."* Julia lays her hands on the water's surface and closes her eyes. She focuses on her hands, but she can only feel the water's movement. She takes a deep breath, trying to concentrate harder.

"I don't feel anything other than the movement." Julia takes another breath, trying

to brush off her frustration. Carmen holds up a finger, telling her to wait. He moves his hands over the water in a circular motion. Slowly, it ripples under his hands, and Julia's eyes light up. He reaches his hand into the water, pulling out a small sphere of water. The water ball is pinched between his thumb and middle finger like he is handling a fragile glass ball.

"Put your hands near the water, feel my energy, and take it from me." Carmen slowly wades through the water closer to Julia. She takes a deep breath and puts her hand near the sphere. She moves around it, feeling a strange pull against her hand. Carmen can see the twinkle in her eye; he knows she can feel the energy flowing. "Now take it." Julia turns her hand and places all her fingers against the sphere. A tingle travels down her arm. She pulls her hand back with a small inhale, keeping her fingers on the water. Her eyes grow wide as Carmen's fingers pull back; she is in complete control of the water. She turns her hand from side to side, baffled this is actually happening.

"Now, the hard part is keeping that energy without touching the water." Carmen picks up another small rock and holds it out. "Take this rock from me using the water."

Julia steps back and extends her arm. With a big exhale, she pulls her fingers from the water. Slowly, she flattens her hand and pushes it towards the water as if pushing it away. She can feel the energy extend from her hand through the air to the water. She smiles big and lets out a small laugh of excitement, and the water drops, splashing back into the river. Julia's smile fades as she stands there, staring at the water in defeat.

"That was amazing!" Carmen yells; Julia shoots a puzzled look at him. "My first did not go that well. I could barely hold the water, let alone move it from my hand. It took a lot of practice."

Julia smiles, feeling a little better about her attempt. "I can't believe I just did that. I never knew I was capable of anything like that." Julia smiles as she waves her hand over the water, feeling its energy again. She can see small ripples as her hand passes over it.

Julia spends the next hour practicing moving the water. Carmen shows off juggling water balls and throws them up for Cypress to catch. Water has always been his strength, but he has never had the kind of control that he does in this world. Not that he'd admit that to Julia. Even last night, lighting the fire, it came more naturally to him than ever before. Carmen is enjoying his newfound strength and control over his power.

"I think this is enough practice today. How about we make some lunch? I'm pretty sure I caught a rabbit in one of my traps."

Carmen nods as the two of them get out of the water. Julia hands Carmen the towel she had pulled from one of the bags. She takes a second one, wrapping it around herself.

Tying it around his waist, he put his clothes into the extra bag, and they head back to where they camped the night before. Julia trails off to one of her traps to see if she caught anything. Carmen sets up the fire and puts as much energy as he can into getting the fire extra hot. They will need to cook and eat fast. It is already noon, and they need to head out soon to make it through the Dragon Forest before dusk.

Julia mentioned it would only be an hour hike, but they need to be clear of the area well before any dragons wake up. Carmen finds a large flat stone and props it above the fire. He can already feel the stone getting extremely hot. Julia comes back with an already-skinned rabbit. Carmen's eyes grow wide; he didn't expect her to have it ready so quickly.

"Since we don't have much time, I'm just going to cut off what we need, and Cypress will eat the rest; raw rabbit is his favorite." Cypress' ears perk up at the sound of his name. He had fallen asleep next to the warmth of the fire, but even fast-asleep food caught his interest. His tail wags excitedly as Julia cuts off small chunks to cook for her and Carmen. She places them on the stone, and there is an instant sizzle. Tossing the rest of the rabbit to the side, Cypress jumps at it and starts digging in. Julia walks over to the bag and pulls out some berries, crushing them up she drains the juice onto the stone. Carefully using her fingers, she rolls the meat over the berry juice bubbling from the heat. It doesn't take long for the meat to finish cooking, allowing them to eat.

Julia finishes eating first, grabs her clothes from her bag, and gets dressed. Carmen quickly finishes and gets dressed as well. Once dressed, Carmen kicks the stone over the fire. Julia watches intently as he starts waving his hand over the fire. She can see a small dome of smoke forming over the fire, the smoke whips and whirls inside. The fire is slowly getting snuffed out. Julia watches closely as she notices little orange sparks extending from Carmen's fingers onto the outside of the dome. Suddenly, inside the dome, there is a big roar of fire. The sparks connect, and with a loud whoosh, the fire and smoke travel up the sparks and into Carmen's fingers. Julia notices the puzzled look on Carmen's face.

"That was super awesome! I wonder if I can do that, too!" Julia jumps with excitement. She wonders why Carmen seems concerned. The whole power thing is new to her, and she can't understand what is wrong with what just happened.

"That wasn't supposed to happen. I was just using the air to snuff out the fire, and somehow, I absorbed the fire's energy. Powers like that don't exist where I come from, so I have no clue what that was."

Julia walks over to Carmen, placing a hand on his shoulder.

"That's what makes you special, and you know what, I like special things."

Carmen cracks a light smile as he rolls his head in her direction. He feels weak, unable to control his powers, but he doesn't want Julia to see.

Julia whistles for Cypress, who perched himself in a tree to sleep after he finished his rabbit. He stretches a little before letting his body fall from the branch. Julia jumps to catch him; she shakes a finger at him in disappointment. Cypress just yawns and curls back to sleep in her arms. Carefully, she stuffs him into the empty space in Carmen's bag. She pulls the drawstrings of the bag to hide him. She wants to ensure he's hidden and asleep so he won't make any noises and accidentally expose them to the other dragons. Julia and Carmen follow a trail for about five miles before Carmen notices the thickening forest. There is a heavy smog that fills the air around them. The smell of sulfur bites at their noses, making it hard for them to breathe. They pull their shirts over their mouths to help filter the air. The sounds of low grumbles and random bursts of air surround them. The two try walking as quickly and quietly as possible, but the thick air makes breathing hard, slowing them down. Julia stops, crouching low to the ground. She pants quickly, trying to catch her breath. Although not much better, the air lower to the ground is slightly better quality and cooler.

"It's been so long since I've traveled here that I forgot how bad the air was." Julia says covering her face with her shirt to filter the air.

Carmen kneels down beside her. He places one hand on her back and the other in front of her face. He waves his hand around. The smog whirls around and clears from in front of her face. Carmen leans his face close to hers, and they take some slow, deep breaths.

"Try to feel the energy. There isn't a lot of clean air, but we can at least thin the smog."

Julia reaches up, placing her hand next to Carmen. She tries to feel the energy of the air but can only feel his hand near hers. Slowly, she moves her hand closer to Carmen until they are touching. As their hands touch, orange sparks appear. Julia tries to pull back quickly, but it is too late. There is a loud, roaring flash of light. Carmen and Julia cover their eyes as they are thrown back. Carmen rolls off his back as Cypress lets out a loud yelp. He pulls the bag around him to the front, holding it tight to his chest to try to comfort Cypress. The air is thick with smoke from the explosion, and Carmen can't see as his eyes are watering and burning. Covering his mouth, he feels around to look for Julia. He can hear her coughing and wheezing.

"Julia, are you ok? I can't see you." Carmen shouts in a whisper, trying to still be quiet. Julia's only response is more coughing and light groans. Trying to look through the smoke, Carmen notices little flashes of light in the distance, followed by roars and screeches. Panic sets in as he realizes the sounds and flashes are getting closer. They woke up some dragons. *Julia, say something so I can find you! We need to go!"* Carmen screams, wasting no time trying to be quiet.

"I'm over here," Julia yells back as loud as possible, causing her to cough louder. Carmen turns around to follow the sound of her voice; he must have passed her. Carmen's frustration grows with each step. This smoke needs to clear. He swings the bag back around to his back. He takes a deep breath and shoves his hands forward with an aggressive exhale. Air shoots from his hands, pushing the smoke back. He pushes harder with another deep breath and exhales out, thinning the smoke. Just a few feet in front of him, Julia is kneeling

on the ground, covering her eyes. Her hands are covered in blood. Carmen freezes in fear. On the other side of Julia is a giant dragon. It is long and slender with a giraffe-like neck. It is covered in red and black scales. Slowly, the dragon flashes a large smile, revealing rows of yellow jagged teeth. A long snake-like tongue pokes out as the dragon licks its lips. The ground shakes beneath them as three more dragons stomp behind it. Two large dragons and a small one. The two larger dragons look identical. Both have large, bulky bodies with bright green and black scales. The smaller dragon seems younger with a slim, scrawny figure. It has blue and purple scales with spots of black fuzz on its tail and a round belly that hasn't fallen off yet. Trembling, Carmen slowly bends down, extending a hand towards Julia.

"Julia, we need to get going."

Julia reaches for his hand before slowly pulling back. She can feel the presence of the dragons behind her. She turns around slowly as she gets back to her feet.

"Back up slowly, I'm right here." Carmen's voice is soft.

Julia can't move, her feet frozen. She slowly looks up at four beasts towering over her. Fear runs through her. The dragons' mouths pull back into a big smile as they lick their lips, ready to feast.

"Where are you off to my Tasty's? No need to rush; you just got here. Stay awhile....... relax." The head dragon's voice booms. She waves her long, scaly arms to the side. "My children assist our guests to the den and make them comfortable." The two larger dragons crouch to the ground, prowling around either side to surround Carmen and Julia. The smaller dragon stays behind, letting out a low growl as it hopes from side to side with excitement. Carmen feels a stir in his bag. Quickly, he pulls the straps to his side to tighten the bag, trying to keep

Cypress from getting out. He reaches forward with his free hand and pulls Julia's arm. He winces slightly, hoping there isn't another explosion. Julia turns, pulling away from Carmen's hand. Smoothly, she slips the bow from her back, the arrow following as she settles it into the bow. Faster than he can follow, the arrow shoots off, grazing the side of the head dragon's face. Julia starts running back through the opening between the dragons. The head dragon lets out a loud roar as she slaps a paw on her bleeding cheek.

"Get them! I want my snack!" The two larger dragons lunge after them to attack. The smaller one stays behind, screeching while jumping from side to side. Carmen and Julia run as fast as possible, dodging fireballs and claws. Both dragons fly above, swatting at them. Julia and Carmen split up, trying to ward off the dragons. Carmen runs frantically, afraid for his and Cypress's lives; he feels a tingle on his hip. He glances down quickly to see the sword handle glowing orange. With a

swift motion, he stops abruptly, spinning his body around. With all his trust in the sword handle, he swings it out from his hip. As his body twists, a long blade extends out with a loud *shing*. The dragon on his tail pulls back as the blade nicks its face. It wails loudly in pain. At that moment, a crazy idea pops into Carmen's head.

"Julia, does this sword do the same little trick your arrow does," Carmen shouts into the woods.

"I don't know," Julia screams back.

"I guess we're about to find out," he exclaims.

In a last-ditch effort to save them, he terrifyingly throws the blade with all his strength at the dragon. It whizzes through the air with lightning speed, slicing into the dragon's chest. With a hard thud, the dragon's body slams into the ground. Carmen reaches his hand out as the sword flies back to him. He looks at the sword in hand, astonished at what just happened. He looks around for Julia and the other dragon. She must have kept running as the other dragon went after her. He hears a roar of fire and bolts in the direction it came from to find her.

Julia keeps wiping blood from her face as she runs frantically. Luckily, the tree cover is thick, so she can dodge the fireballs being hurled at her. All of a sudden, Julia trips on a tree stump. She rolls to her back to see the large dragon hovering over her. It hesitates for a moment, giving her a smile of victory. Julia starts hyperventilating as the dragon opens its mouth and shoots one last victorious fireball at her. She lets out a loud, high-pitched screech. Sound waves echo from Julia's mouth. The dragon is thrown back against a tree. It falls to the ground, whimpering in pain, holding its long ears from the deafening screech. Carmen catches up to Julia, picking her up off the ground. Cypress, who had been wiggling around in the bag, finally breaks free. He lets out a loud squeal, seeing Julia in Carmen's arms bleeding. As he tries to lick her face, he notices the dragon whimpering on the ground. Rage sparks in Cypress as he flies over to the other dragon, letting out little roars. With each roar, a small burst of fire shoots out, striking the other dragon and making it whimper more. It has lost all energy to fight even a baby dragon-like Cypress. The large dragon jumps up and flies off faster than Cypress can. He retreats to Carmen and Julia, who proudly watch his bravery. Still in Carmen's arms, Julia snatches Cypress out of the air and holds him tight to her chest. Carmen hugs them both tight as he pushes himself forward to escape the area. He huffs as his arms ache under Cypress' added weight. He tenses his arms more, holding them as tight as he can. He doesn't want to stick around for more dragons to show up. Julia lets Carmen carry her for a bit before jumping down and running on her own. Cypress flies around with them as he is too heavy for her to carry on her own and he is too anxiously worked up to go back in the bag. They don't talk for a few miles to not alert other dragons to their trespassing. They make it to the edge of the woods as the trees begin to thin out. Julia tosses her bag against a tree, sinking down against a rock. She lets out a big sigh. She casually holds up her hand, letting out a loud whistle. There is a long silence until the arrow whizzes through the air back to her hand. She stuffs it back into her quiver.

"Why are you stopping? They will get us; what if they come after us in larger numbers." Carmen looks around frantically, making sure they aren't being followed. He holds the sword tight in his hands, turning to inspect in all directions. Realizing the coast is clear, his shoulders relax, and the blade retracts into the handle. He fastens it to his hip while kneeling beside Julia, pulling a cloth from her bag. He wraps it around her head to cover the still bleeding gouges. She pushes his hands away and pulls out a baggie of now crushed Valetudo berries.

"We crossed out of Dragon Forest a half mile back. They can't harm us off their land unless we harm them." Julia reaches back into her bag to pull out a small metal teapot. She gestures for Carmen to make a fire. He takes the pot from her hand and kicks around some twigs on the ground.

"I killed one of them with my sword." Carmen hesitates for a moment before picking up the sticks he had been kicking at. Julia rolls her eyes and digs more in her bag for something else.

"First off, I wouldn't have stopped if it meant we were still in danger. I do know what I am doing and am stronger than you know. I will not be treated like some damsel that needs saving." Carmen stands still, speechless. Cypress perches up in a tree, focusing on the woods they just came from.

"Secondly, I'm sorry to say, but you didn't kill it. Dragons heal extremely fast. Unless its *heart came out with the sword, it'll be fine. Their bodies merely go into a coma-like state until they repair themselves. Third, Dragons are cursed to harm no one off their lands. The kings designated the forest as a safe haven for dragons to bring peace between them and humans. They'll burn up and die if they harm anyone outside the Dragon Forest."* Julia flips her hair back with a hard sigh; she notices her anger flaring as she takes a deep breath to calm herself. She isn't angry with him; she is just confused and hurt. The idea of someone helping her is different. She is used to being alone with no one to help or make her feel better. Her strength and independence make her feel invincible. Yet somehow, depending on Carmen makes her feel weak. It is frustrating yet freeing to have someone else who cares. Carmen is going home; she keeps reminding herself that she won't have this forever.

"I am so sorry I offended you. I meant nothing by it. I know you are strong, brave, and brilliant. You're an amazing being. I was just scared to lose you."

Julia's eyes grow wide as Carmen's face grows red. She sighs again, throwing her face into her hands.

"What the fuck was that sonic scream! It was truly amazing!" Carmen kneels down, trying again to hand her the cloth from her bag, hoping to relieve some tension. She pulls her head back, giving him a smile. She takes the cloth and wipes the dried blood off her face.

Carmen finishes setting up the sticks for a fire as Cypress drops down from the trees, prancing at Carmen's side. Carmen backs away, waving his hand and motioning Cypress to start the fire. Cypress lets out an excited squeal, and his nose pours out smoke. Quickly, he draws his head back, opening his mouth. Jerking his head forward, he shoots out the smallest spark of fire, missing the branches. He wiggles his nose, groaning. Carmen laughs as Cypress takes a deep breath and lunges his head forward in another attempt. This time, a

small fireball shoots out, igniting the branches.
Julia and Carmen clap excitedly as he jumps
around, squealing with his head held high. They
laugh at him, prancing around with joy.
Carmen places the pot of berries on the fire to
warm it, then sits by Julia against the tree.

*"I do owe you an apology. I was just
overwhelmed and scared. I usually do this
alone, and it's easier when you're only worried
about yourself than two other beings."*

Carmen smiles at her as she hands him the
cloth. She lowers her head to him as he gently
wraps it around her head, covering the wounds.

*"I have no idea where the scream came
from. I felt helpless, and it's not something I'm
used to feeling."* Julia sighs, still watching in
amazement as Cypress continues prancing
around in his triumph. It is such a joy to watch
him grow and change so quickly.

*"Well, Maybe you can recreate it. Try not to
think about the emotion you were feeling but*

the energy you felt when it happened. Emotions play a big part in the strength of our powers, but it's the energy that really brings them to life." Carmen looks at Julia, hopeful. She is capable of much more than either of them realizes. Julia's expression changes to uncertainty.

She doesn't want to recreate the feeling of almost being eaten alive by a dragon. Still, she is intrigued to learn more about her powers.

"I'll try, but no promises. I'm still trying to relax from everything." Julia gets up slowly and turns to face a thick patch of trees. She takes a slow, deep breath, focusing on the feeling of the air as it passes her lips, over her tongue, and into her throat. She can feel her lungs fill, the energy moving within. She forces the air out hard, letting out a straining scream. Carmen covers his ears as Cypress shrieks, flying off into the woods to hide behind a tree. Julia rolls her eyes and sighs as she clears her throat for another try. She takes another deep

breath, focusing on the feeling. She holds her breath for a moment, clenching her fist. She can feel her lungs tensing as they struggle to hold air. She counts to three and lets out another scream. This time, she doesn't force it out; she just lets the air out of her lungs naturally as she focuses on the energy within the air as she screams. The trees in front of her bend back, their roots gripping the ground, hanging on for dear life before de-rooting into a big pile. Julia lets out a shriek as she jumps up and down with excitement. Carmen smiles wide as Julia leaps at him, falling into his arms for a hug.

"See, absolutely amazing! It's funny you haven't discovered them earlier."

Julia pulls back from their embrace. She focuses on his smile, tilting her head and letting her hair cover her face.

How had she not discovered these powers even by accident? She can't even recall mysterious incidents or anything strange that might have happened. Maybe Carmen being here had unlocked something in her. Perhaps she needed the balance of strength and weakness to unleash these unknown powers. She shakes her head to breathe from the confusion her head is spiraling into.

"Yeah, I am pretty awesome." She gives Carmen a wink and lets out a giggle. "I feel bad for the next dumb ass who wants to fuck with me." A huge smile stretches across her face. She rolls to the side, resting her head in Carmen's lap, looking up at the sky through the treetops. He brushes his hand through her hair as they look up at the stars. Moments of silence pass, and they're interrupted by a loud whistle. They both jump. They had forgotten the teapot on the fire. Carmen jumps up, rushing over to the fire. He pours the tea into a cup, handing it off to Julia. She sits against the tree, brushing her hair out of her face before chugging the tea. "May I have some more, please? I should probably drink the whole pot to heal my head."

Carmen nods as he turns back to the fire. After pouring another cup he restocks the fire with a few more sticks.

"So, where are we heading tomorrow? Hopefully, it's nowhere deadly. I think I need a break from danger for a day."

Julia and Carmen laugh at the idea. Julia takes the cup from Carmen again, taking a big gulp of tea.

"Tomorrow will be nice and easy. We're headed for a little town called Dracfall. We need to stop there so I can stock up on some food and supplies. Hunting isn't turning up enough food for us, especially since Cypress grows larger each day." Julia says with a half smile. She winces as Carmen sits behind her, trying to comb some more dried blood out of her hair with the carved wooden comb he found in the bag. He dips the comb in some water and gently combs through her hair, trying to smooth it down.

Julia sips her tea as she sits staring at the fire. She smiles big, knowing Carmen can't see her face. He is so gentle, trying not to pull her hair. It is sweet and feels so nice on her scalp. Once he finishes Julia's hair, the two sit together, enjoying the fire and watching Cypress test his new fire breath. Slowly, over time, Julia notices Carmen closing his eyes and falling asleep. She stays up, watching him sleep. She tilts her head, admiring how perfect he looks even as he sleeps. His black hair is still neat and kept as if they hadn't been through a rough day. She is happy that Carmen has come into her life. He gives her hope that her life can be better. She frowns for a moment. In just a few days, he will return to his home, and she will have to return to her lonely life at her cabin. At least she will always have Cypress by her side. She slowly drifts off to sleep alongside Carmen. Laying back, her head rests against his chest. The sound of his heartbeat soothes her to sleep. Cypress flies down from the trees, trying to nestle between

them like the night before, but there isn't
enough room, so he opts to sleep at Julia's feet.

121

Growing Connections

In the morning, Carmen awakes wanting to attempt making Julia breakfast as a thanks for all she has done. He grabs Julia's bag and pulls out the containers of rabbit Julia had smoked the previous day, along with some sausage. *What would a breakfast be without eggs?* he thinks, venturing into the woods. He heads towards the river hoping to quickly find his way back. He focuses on the treetops scanning for a nest. *Was this even the season for birds to lay eggs? Would there be any birds in the area?* He shakes his head, trying to stay positive. He spots a tall tree with a nest at the river's edge. The branches start low on the tree, so it will be easy for him to climb. As he approaches the nest, he sees the mother bird inside. She is a medium-sized bird with tail feathers varying shades of blue and red. Her beak is long and sharp with two brown dots for the nose. Ever so slowly, Carmen reaches for the bird. She lets out a loud screech, pecking at Carmen to scare him off. He swats at her with one hand while using the other to cling to the tree. In defeat, she flies off, abandoning her eggs in the nest. He takes the eggs, placing them in him shirt that he has pulled up to carry them. He's shocked to see twelve eggs in the nest. In his universe, this is very uncommon; birds only lay two or three eggs at a time. Things here are so similar but also very different.

He hurries back to the camp, carefully putting the eggs in a small basket beside the fire. There are so many eggs he has to gently stack them over the top so they won't fall. He begins cooking the sausage and pieces of rabbit. He waves for Cypress to come over; he has excitedly been watching Carmen since he got back. He whispers to Cypress that he should blow some fire onto the coals from the night before to get more heat under the stone. He tosses fresh sticks on the coals as Cypress blows fire under the stone; the coals and sticks crackle and sizzle. Cracking the eggs on the stone, he carefully stirs them, ensuring they don't roll to the ground. Julia's food needs to be perfect when he brings it to her. Julia wakes to the sweet aroma of what Carmen is put together. She rolls over with a large stretch, facing Carmen with a big grin. In his hand is a plate filled with food. It has three eggs, four pieces of sausage, and some rabbit strips. She sits up with a big smile.

"Mmmm, this smells so good. Should I prepare for the worst? Most princes don't know how to cook." Julia giggles as she reaches for the plate. Carmen pulls the plate back, sticking his head up.

"Oh well, I guess you're not hungry. I am capable of more than you know." Carmen looks back at her with a big smile, mocking her own words from earlier. Quickly, she shakes her head and extends her arms with grabby hands in a childlike manner. Carmen chuckles as he gives her the plate. Their hands brush slightly against each other, the orange spark dancing around their hands. They look into each other's eyes, pausing for a moment. It has only been a few days since they met, but they both feel that meeting each other was more than a happy accident. It feels like it was always meant to happen. Something just feels right between them. The kind of feeling you can't quite explain, but neither of them are willing to voice these feelings to each other as they don't want their new friendship to be awkward.

Carmen's cheeks turn red as he pulls away and rushes back to the campfire to finish making breakfast for himself and Cypress. While cooking his breakfast, he thinks about these feelings for Julia. She is smart, funny, caring, and the most beautiful young woman he has ever laid eyes on. He is beyond happy and thankful to have met her. But he isn't sure how she feels about him, so he's trying to brush it off. He can't stay here with her, and she certainly won't want to leave her home and go with him; she's too independent to ever want that.

Carmen picks at the food as it cooks; he's not super hungry, and Cypress is a growing dragon who needs all the energy he can get. He calls Cypress over for his meal, putting it in a large bowl. He gives him the rest of what is left, hoping it will fill his belly. After serving Cypress' meal, he packs their bags, cleaning everything up. He leaves Julia and Cypress to eat their food while walking to the river for a quick bath to clean himself.

He stays in the water for a few moments, swimming around and enjoying his time relaxing. It is nice to have a moment to breathe, relax, and clear his mind, which is filled with so many questions, emotions, and worries. It is like the river is just carrying all those overwhelming thoughts and feelings away. Carmen gets out of the water to rejoin the others, knowing Julia might be done with her food by now; he doesn't want her to come looking for him. Carmen gets out of the water and realizes he forgot to grab a towel to dry off. He doesn't want to put on his clothes while soaking wet. He grabs a branch with an abundance of leaves and uses it to cover himself. He runs back to camp, but Julia isn't there. He lets out a sigh of relief, quickly grabs a towel, and runs back to the river to retrieve his clothes. Throwing the branch of leaves to the side, he tightly secures the towel around his waist. As he approaches the river to grab his clothes, he is startled by a noise. He looks over to the water to see Julia staring at him. She lets out a giggle. He freezes in place; he wasn't expecting her to be here. They didn't pass each other in the woods. Carmen's face turns red when he realizes he's staring.

"I knew you were shy." She giggles, mocking his embarrassment. Carmen shakes his head, trying to think of a quick response.

"No, I-I-I just didn't see you pass me, so it caught me off guard, that's all." Julia tilts her head, pressing her lips together,while raising an eyebrow at him. Her arms cross in front of her, pushing up her chest, waiting for him to come up with another lie. Carmen stammers before quickly snatching up his clothes and running back to camp. Julia giggles, watching his butt tense through the towel as he runs. She washes up quickly so as not to keep Carmen waiting.

Carmen and Cypress are waiting, ready to go when she returns to camp. *"Feel clean now?"* Carmen asks, trying to brush off his embarrassment from earlier. Julia giggles and walks over to grab her bag.

"I feel much cleaner… You know, I never realized you tense your butt when you run until today." Julia winks as she pushes by him. She isn't going to let him off that easily. Carmen blushes and grabs his bag, running to catch up with her. They walk together in awkward silence. To break the tension, Carmen thinks it would be a good idea to practice their powers;

they toss back and forth a rock and a ball of water.

It is fun for a bit, but Julia loses interest and decides she wants to learn more about Carmen. She asks a million and one questions about his home, family, and friends. She asks him about possible girlfriends and ex-girlfriends. Faced with embarrassment again, Carmen tries brushing those questions off and directs the conversation to how much Cypress has grown in the last few days.

Cypress has gotten sleepy, so Carmen attempts to put him in the bag to sleep, but he won't fit anymore. Carmen ends up carrying him for a while. Julia points out that he has started losing his fur, and some scales are coming in. His coloring is odd to Julia; most dragons only have a few colored scales; however, Cypress has many. He has red, blue, green, and purple. He even has a few white ones, which aren't typical for dragons. As Carmen brushes his hand across Cypress, little fur clumps come out in his hand, revealing more scales. Julia explains that a dragon's scale color usually indicates their abilities. Cypress having firepower means he should be black with red and green. Carmen questions what Cypress' various colored scales mean, but Julia has no idea. Carmen and Julia continue talking for hours as they walk.

Talking is coming naturally to them now, with no lulls or awkward silences. Occasionally, Julia will shush him mid-conversation to have him listen or show him the different birds and animals she likes. They are similar to the animals in his universe, but he will gladly listen to her talk all day. He adores how her eyes light up, hoping she is helping him discover something new. They talk about their universes.

For the most part, they are exactly the same, with a few minor differences. They question the minor differences. *Like the lack of dragons in Carmen's universe, did his people kill them instead of making deals with them? Is that why they are folk tales rather than reality? Or the way magic in Julia's world works. Does everyone actually have powers and just lack the knowledge to use them? These tangents went on and on like old friends catching up.*

After a good rest, Cypress happily flies around and plays fireball catch with himself in the trees as he follows along. Every now and again, he would fling one at Carmen waiting for him to fling it back. This amuses Cypress greatly and becomes a fun game for him. He generally spends his time up in the trees. He likes being high up in the sky feeling the wind on his wings, only coming down when he gets scared of an animal making noise or needs a nap. The duration of his naps is getting shorter than when they started their journey. When Cypress gets excited he rushes down pointing with excited squeaks and squeals.

Dracfalls

Cautiously, they approach the tree line. They are up high, overlooking a large valley with a little village in the center. The village circles around a large pond fed from the river they've been following. On one side is a farm with children running and playing with animals. To the other, houses, a school, and a tall pointed building that looks like a church or town hall. Carmen and Julia descend down the hill through the long grass to Dracfalls.

Julia points out a small lodge next to the local market. *"They should have a room for us to stay the night while we gather supplies. They don't get a lot of visitors here."*

Carmen nods as he lowers his eyebrows at her. *"Don't we need some form of payment to stay? I imagine we can't stay without giving something in return."*

Julia smiles. *"I've got that covered. I have coins in my bag; I keep them hidden in a secret pocket. My parents were pretty wealthy. I don't pay for my house or the land it's on. The king gave it to me when my parents passed. My father was the king's most trusted knight. When he passed, the king felt bad for me and wanted to make sure I was all set."*

Carmen tilts his head in confusion. *What kind of king gives a little girl a home without making sure she is being cared for?* He continues following her to the Lodge without asking the question out loud.

The Lodge is large inside, with a bar on the backside and empty tables scattered around. They approach the bar, knocking on the counter. An old lady burst through the doors behind the bar to greet them. They inform her they need a place to spend the night. The lady nods and disappears through the set of doors behind the bar. They hear whispering before a tall, wrinkly old man walks out from the doors. He has dark rings under his eyes; they're almost black with a thin blue ring surrounding the darkness. His hair is long and wiry. It has an aged salt-and-pepper look with some brown highlights peeking through. It looks like he hasn't washed it in weeks. His fingers are long and crooked with long, yellow, unkept nails. He taps them on the countertop while flashing his crooked yellow grin at them. Julia cringes in disgust at the man's appearance. She hasn't seen him before. She reaches back, nervously grabbing Carmen's hand.

"Welcome traveler to the Dracfalls Lodge. My name is Simon. I hear you're looking for a place to stay. We have a room available for you, but it is rather small for three." His voice is high and scratchy as he speaks with his breath. He leans over to Julia, breathing in her face. His breath smells like uncooked liver that has been sitting out for weeks. Julia pulls back against Carmen. Cypress steps forward, snorting smoke into the man's face as if to say back off. *"What a lovely dragon. I hope he's friendly."* The man frowns wider as he leans back.

"Yes, he is quite friendly. The size of the room doesn't matter; it will only be for the night." Carmen speaks sternly to him. Simon continues gazing awkwardly at Julia.

"Very well then. The room available is in the building across the street. It has some furniture but not a lot of it. If you need anything, Mary can help you." Julia extends a hand forward with some coins. He pushes her hand back, curling his long fingers around her hand. A wide smile stretches across his face. "No need for payment. Seeing a pretty face like yours around here is enough. It's not often we see anything other than hags." Simon lets out a strained laugh that turns into a cough. Julia rips her hand back from his grip as Carmen glares at him.

"Thank you," Julia says with hesitation. They walk backward, keeping an eye on Simon. He waves them away and vanishes through the doors. Cypress locks his position, glaring before following Carmen and Julia out of the building. Outside, they're greeted by a short, round woman with medium brown hair. She has

a bright smile with the brightest green eyes.
She wears a long plaid dress with a brown
apron over it.

"Hi, my name is Mary. I am Simon's
assistant. I will be showing you to your room.
Feel free to wander around while enjoying your
stay." Her big smile now seems fake. Julia
frowns at her, she doesn't recognize her either.
Mary just keeps smiling; none of them reply. As
they follow Mary, Cypress keeps his head low,
sniffing at her feet to keep an eye on her. He
has a feeling of discomfort about the people in
this town. Things seemed so nice from the top
of the valley, but now it looks dark and eerie.
The sky became gray with clouds, and the kids
playing are no where be seen. Julia can tell by
watching him closely that something is off.

When they get to the room, Mary waves
them in with the same fake smile, then vanishes
with a slam of the door. Carmen and Julia just
stare at each other before examining the room.
The room, as Simon described it, is very small.
It has a half bed with only one pillow and a

small round table with two chairs. On the table is a single candle covered with melted wax with no wick left to burn. The room is musty, dusty and crusty; it looks like it has never been cleaned.

"It's better than the hard ground." Carmen shrugs, trying to make light of the situation. Julia shrugs back as she unpacks their bags to make a list of supplies she needs. Carmen offers to help, but Julia brushes him off. She suggests he take Cypress to the field to play fireball toss or something. She knows best what they need and what shops will have what she wants as she has been here many times before.

Walking through the village, everyone stares at Carmen and Cypress through their windows like hawks watching prey. It's an eerie feeling. They brush it off as they continue to the field. As they get closer to the field, Carmen can hear the faint cries of a woman, but he can't tell where it's coming from. He looks around frantically as it gets louder. This is the voice he heard when standing guard at the doors. There is a slight tingle in his hands. He looks down to see little orange sparks dancing around his fingers. He examines his hands for a moment. It feels like a warning, but he continues. Cypress walks on, clueless about what Carmen is thinking, as he can't hear the crying.

Carmen notices a random door in the middle of the clearing as they approach the field. The tingling in his hand and the women's cries intensify. Cypress crouches down low, growling as he notices the door. It is large with a tall peak at the top. The slab at the bottom is thick with lots of cracks. It is a plain brown door with large brass plates holding it together. This door looks similar to the 7 located in the Animus Kingdom. Carmen wonders if this is one of the 14 doors he's never seen in the other kingdoms that Domonic had made all those years ago. Carmen snaps his fingers at Cypress, beckoning him back to his side. Cypress pulls back but keeps low, his wings flat, ready to pounce.

Carmen reaches for the doorknob, pulling on it hesitantly. The door flings open with a gust of wind as a loud scream echoes. Carmen falls to the ground, covering his ears. He reaches for the door to push it shut. Panic sets in as he worries that Cypress and himself will get pulled into another unknown universe. Inside the door is a swirling black and green vortex. He looks away, feeling its hypnotic pull on him. His hand connects with the door, and the orange static coming from his hand encases the door. Everything falls silent as the gusts of wind stop. Information floods Carmen's mind, more intense and knowledgeable than any door he's previously opened. It comes with a message from the past. This is the door to the time universe. The vortex clears, only revealing darkness and a green haze. The figure of a man appears, calling out to him.

"Carmen, my boy. You must follow your destiny. You hold great power that will terrify those around you. Don't let it be the reason for your demise, as it was mine. You will do great *things in life, but you will need to make the right choices."*

Carmen recognizes the man from a drawing in one of the books he's read called The Doors of Domonic. The man speaking to him is Domonic. Carmen wonders why Domonic called him *"my boy"*; he has no children. *How does someone who died 200 years ago know his name?*

"Carmen, listen to me closely. Those orange sparks aren't just fun little indicators. They are your-"

Suddenly, Cypress slams the door shut in a panic, cutting off Domonic.

"Nooooo!" Carmen lunges for the door knob to open it, but when he does, it opens to nothing but the field. For a moment, he looks through the empty door. *What does this all mean? Why is this happening to him? What are the orange sparks?* Carmen pushes the door shut for a final time, and it quickly collapses into a pile of ash. A gust of wind takes the ash off into the sky, leaving no trace of the door.

Not even the slab remains. Carmen looks at Cypress, who is just as confused; they turn to quickly make their way back to Julia.

Rushing back through town, not a soul can be seen or heard. Cypress and Carmen look at each other with puzzled looks on their faces. *Where did everyone go?* No one in the windows stalking them. This town keeps getting weirder with each passing minute.

Carmen explains to Cypress that he isn't telling Julia about their encounter. *"How do you explain something you don't even understand yourself?"* To settle their minds from all the weirdness, Carmen coaches Cypress into a plan to sneak up on Julia when they return to the room. As they get closer, they are getting ready to bust through the door and scare her when Julia suddenly jumps up, scaring them.

"Don't you two even think about it! I have eyes in the back of my head. Nothing will get by me." Julia laughs as she hands them a sandwich and walks into the room, shutting the

door behind her. They can hear her beginning to sing; the two stand there astonished. When they finally grasp what happened, they go into the room to eat with Julia. "So, what did you two do at the park?" Julia looks at them with a smile. They look at each other with terrified looks as they tell Julia of their ordeal with the town's people and how eerie and unwelcoming it was. Julia can sense they are hiding something but doesn't push the issue.

"Well, you both seem fine. We will need to be cautious; if anything happens, just yell loudly. This village isn't very big, so it's not hard to hear a loud noise."

Carmen and Cypress gulp and nod simultaneously. Julia lowers her brows at their weirdness but brushes it off.

"After lunch, I want to go shopping. There are some supplies I need to get."

Carmen and Cypress nod again as they stuff their faces. Julia counts some coins and places them in a small bag strapped to her hip. She gives a couple to Carmen.

"If you two happen to venture out and see something you want, help yourself. I'll leave the rest in the bag to keep an eye on it. I'm only taking a little to try and negotiate." Julia kisses Cypress on the head. Carmen leans forward hoping for a kiss as well. Julia pets his forehead and dances out the door.

Carmen and Cypress look at each other in confusion with Julia's uplifting mood. The strangeness doesn't seem to concern her at all. Maybe it's the fact she has been to this village several times before, or perhaps they are the crazy ones and nothing is really wrong.

Julia ventures through the town to the mini shop. She has been here a dozen or so times before. It's one of her favorite shops on the island, and the only one in this village. They always have the best selection and diversity. Although not close to her home, it's always a great adventure for her. As Julia walks she notices many new faces, Just like Mary and Simon, it's giving her an eerie feeling. In fact she hasn't seen anyone she recognizes yet.

Standing outside the small run down shop, she prays to see the regular lady that runs it. The windows are covered in dust from years of street traffic. She hesitates for a moment before opening the door. She can hear murmurs coming from behind her. She looks back only to see an old man and woman sitting on a bench, scowling at her. With a light smile and wave, she shrugs it off and gives the door a hard pull. The inside is very large; it seems larger on the inside of the building than it does on the outside. The rows of shelves are stocked full stretching down the length of the building. The lighting is dim and everything is dusty, not that Julia cares, she is just excited to be at a place where she knows she can get all the supplies on her list. As she wanders the isles, something catches her eye. At the end is a display case; it has something she has seen before but can't remember where or when. The owner of the shop comes over. A small, frail woman with long salt and pepper hair. In her hand, she holds a walking cane with a skull as the handle. Her fingers are wrinkly with age, her arms long and thin, her face is oddly smooth but pale, her eyes are golden brown with heavy dark bags under them.

"It's a beauty, isn't it?" the woman asks in a scratchy but very clear voice. Julia glances at her quickly. She raises an eyebrow, tilting her head. Finally, she recognizes someone, but she looks different. She's never looked this old and tired. Her usual greeting was soft and kind, always followed by some banter about how Julia didn't visit her nearly enough. But this time, she didn't. Maybe she's losing her mind with age? Maybe this wasn't her at all, and she was mistaken?

"Ye-yes, it is. What is it?" Julia asks, trying not to stutter.

"Well, it's an egg. Some say it has mystical powers, and some say it is decoration.

I myself believe it's cursed. I've been trying to sell it, but no one seems interested. You can have it if you'd like." The woman says with an ominous smile. Julia looks at the egg. It is off-white with a yellow hint to it. It has green spirals and loops all over it. There's nothing special about it, but somehow oddly beautiful, so Julia agrees to take it. *"Very well, I will box it up for you, and you can take it when you're finished."* The woman takes the egg to the front counter. She doesn't smile or flinch; she holds the same tired expression.

Julia finishes collecting what she needs and hurries to the front counter. She doesn't want to waste any more time here. Carmen is right, something is off with this place. It isn't what she is used to. It is always a happy place with happy people. She places her things on the counter, only for the women to push them back to her.

"Please just take everything and go, Julia. You need to leave now."

Julia's eyes widen as the chill of her name escapes the woman's lips. She did remember. There is a panic in the woman's eyes.

"It's not safe for you here anymore... Please go." She hands a small wooden box to Julia. She opens it carefully, the strange egg is neatly placed inside. She looks at the woman, scared. *Why is she warning her, and what is happening in this town?* *"Please take this as well. It will help you get out of here faster, but you only get one use. Don't open it until you are in a private place."* She pulls her hand from her pocket, revealing a rolled-up paper wrapped in twine with a wax seal. Julia slowly reaches her hand out to take it but hesitates. *"Julia, please take this gratitude before it's too late. Take your friends and leave."*

Hearing the woman say her name for a second time sends chills down her spine. Something is off, and she doesn't know if she should trust her. Julia grabs the paper and tucks it into her waistband. She nods as she quickly grabs the rest of her things. The woman's head twitches; she has a pained look for a few seconds before it fades back to tiredness.

"Have you found everything you need, girly? Don't forget your egg."

Julia squints at the old lady, expressionless. She changed. She isn't the same person who just spoke seconds ago.

"Thank you for your kindness; it won't go unforgotten." she gives a half smile as she bows her head, almost running to the door. She pulls the door shut behind her as she hurries to the inn. The old couple on the bench still glare at her as she hurries past them. She tries to pay no mind to them.

When she gets to the room, she runs in, slamming the door. She begins stuffing everything hastily into the bags. Carmen and Cypress jump up, giving her a strange look.

"We're leaving now, let's go."Julia packs everything in a panic, a little out of breath from rushing out of the shop. Carmen puts his hand on her arm and looks at her with concern.

"We need to pack and leave now. The woman who owns the shop said we need to leave and we aren't safe here. I have no clue what's happening. It's not the same as I remember. The people are different."Julia pulls her arm forward to move Carmen's hand off her as she continues packing. Carmen hasty grabs their things to help pack their bags. Cypress feels Julia's panic as he paces the floor whimpering.

Once all packed, the three head for the trails. They walk through the village quickly, noticing people coming from between the buildings to follow them. They walk quicker, almost running, trying to lose the slowly growing crowd behind them. Carmen notices that they're approaching the clearing that he and Cypress had visited earlier. Thinking quickly, Carmen urges Julia to turn left. They bolt into an alleyway. Carmen stops turning back to face the village. He firmly stomps his foot to the ground, facing his hands down. The ground beneath his feet begins to rumble. He closes his hands and pulls up hard. There is a loud rumble as a wall of earth rises from the ground, blocking the opening between the buildings. He turns, running to catch up with Julia and Cypress. He knows it won't hold them off, but it will reroute the mob, giving the three of them time to get out of the valley. They rush up the hill, and Cypress flies ahead faster than they can run.

Julia stops at the top of the hill just outside the valley and looks back. Breathing hard, she places a hand on a nearby tree. She whistles as Carmen and Cypress run ahead. They stop turning on their heels. Feeling Julia's relief, Cypress plops his body to the ground, panting. Carmen walks over to Julia's side, placing a hand on her shoulder. He can see the village people standing at the edge of the small town. They can't follow them any further.

"They aren't following us. I wonder why." Carmen pulls out his cantina and chugs some water. Julia reaches out a hand, signaling her turn for the water. "What's that on your side?" Carmen notices the paper in Julia's waistband as she reaches for the water. She holds out a finger as she gulps the water.

"The lady at the shop gave this to me. She told me it would help get me out of here but not to open it until I was in a private place."

Carmen frowns slightly, concerned about anything coming from the village. Julia pulls the paper out and unravels the twine. As she unrolls the paper, they realize it's a map. Carmen rolls his eyes as they already have several maps.

Julia's eyes widen as she reads it. "This is a map to the portal dragon, but these paths aren't on my map."

Carmen leans in to look at the map.

"It must be a really old one. These paths don't exist anymore. I would know about them." She notices the outer edge of the map is written in an old language that died out centuries ago. Julia turns the map in circles, reading the writing on the edges. Carmen tries to read along, but he doesn't recognize the language. He waits patiently as she reads it over and over. *"The map says to wave your hand over it and say your destination."*

They look at each other for a moment and wave Cypress over. Carmen smiles big with excitement. *Is this his ticket home? Is it really this simple?*

Carmen waves his hand over the map. *"I want to go to my home in Animus Kingdom."* For a moment, nothing but silence falls around them. They all sit there bummed at the failed attempt. Carmen reaches his hand out to try again.

A big swirling portal forms on the map. As it grows, they step back out of the way. They look into it with amazement. The portal is black with grays and whites swirling in it. Carmen steps towards it only to turn and reach a hand out to Julia. She steps back slightly and grabs Cypress' paw.

"Julia, come with me? You and Cypress can live with me in the castle." Carmen motions her to come with him.

Julia looks at him for a moment, but before she can reply, they are sucked into the portal. As they fall through the darkness, Cypress flails and squeals, freaking out trying to control his flight. Strips of white and gray flash by them, blinding them. All of a sudden, they land on the ground. Carmen lands first as Julia follows, landing on top of him. They try to sit up a little as Cypress follows on top of them. Carmen rubs his head as he lays there for a moment. Julia jumps up in a panic, stammering to find words. Carmen sits up, realizing her panic; they're back in the room.

"How did we end up back here!" Julia quickly darts to the windows to pull the curtains shut. She peeks out, making sure no one's watching or sees them. She gasps as she sees the whole village standing outside the inn. *"She lied to me. She wanted to make sure we would be brought back here to them if we got away."*

"Maybe not. You said she mentioned a safe way to get out of here. Maybe it has to be used from within the village to work. She was warning you to leave. Why would she betray you?" Carmen looks around for the map frantically. It's nowhere to be found.

Julia shakes her head. *"Maybe, I don't know, everything is so different and weird."* She pushes against the door, holding it in place as fists pound against it, trying to break their way in. Carmen bolts over to help her keep it shut.

"We need to get out of here." Carmen looks around the room for an idea. Cypress

cowers in the corner of the room at Julia's feet. *"I have an idea, but you need to trust me. I will blast the door open with air. It will only take them a second to realize what's happening. We can run and make our way to the field. Cypress, you can fly off to get away. At the field, the ground will be softer; I can try to carry you with me. My powers have been getting stronger. I know I can do it."*

Julia looks at Carmen, worry growing in her eyes. For a moment, she looks between him and Cypress before nodding.

"Please don't drop me!" her eyes plead at him.

He smiles big as he backs away from the door. *"I won't, I promise."*

Still unsure, Julia gives him a half smile as she jumps back from the door. Carmen pulls his arms back and jams them forward. A big gust of wind pushes the door open, causing dust and sand to fly through the air. The three-bolt out of the room, listening to the villagers coughing and choking on the particles in the air. Running down the pathway, they look back at the villagers who caught on after the dust settled.

"We need to get to the field where the ground is softer," Carmen yells over the shouts of the crowd chasing them. Julia nods as she runs faster. As they approach the opening for the field, Simon steps out from an alleyway blocking their path.

Behind him, follow two men. Cypress flies up and over to the field. Carmen pulls Julia back as she wraps her arms around him. Facing his palms down, he clenches his hand into a fist and pulls it up hard. The ground rumbles and shifts slightly under their feet. This isn't the soft ground Carmen hoped for, but he needs to try. The men charge after them with a single point from Simon. Julia closes her eyes, not wanting to watch everyone coming at them from either direction. Carmen throws his hands down again, then pulls up hard. This time, the earth brokes free beneath them. The two rise up in the air, Julia clenches her eyes shut even tighter. She's afraid to look. Carmen smiles big as he can see Cypress in the distance. He's doing it, and he's catching up with Cypress! He would never want to harm Julia, but he had no idea if he could actually pull this off. He's carried himself before for a short amount of time but never another person. He remembers all his failed attempts when he first arrived and clenches his fist tighter.

On the ground, Simon grunts and stomps his foot. He storms over to the two men standing there dumbfounded.

"I want you two to go and find me the twins. Seeing as you two can't do the simplest of tasks, I want the twins to kill the 3 of them. I originally wanted the dragon alive to use him as a mule, but he's too loyal to them; it'll never do as I command." He smacks both men upside the head before heading back to the Lodge.

Friends or Foes?

Cypress finds a sturdy tree to perch in as Carmen gently lands him and Julia on the ground. When she feels the earth settling under her feet, she opens an eye to make sure they're actually on the ground. She lets out a big sigh; she has been holding her breath the whole time. Carmen laughs as he hugs her tightly.

"Thank you for not dropping me." Julia squeezes back. They embrace for a moment. Cypress flies down from the trees and snuggles against them. Julia grunts as she struggles to pick him up and holds him between them. "You did great, buddy. You did so well, my brave boy."

Cypress rubs his head against her chest, letting out a little squeak. After a few moments of hugging, Cypress starts wiggling from boredom. Carmen and Julia laugh as he finds entertainment by kicking a pinecone on the ground. Julia starts heading through the woods with Carmen behind her. They walk for a few miles before Cypress starts lagging behind. They decide to stop for the night to get some rest. They had lost track of time, with how crazy everything got. The sky is clear, with a warm breeze blowing about. Carmen and Julia opt to sleep under the stars so they don't have to set up a canopy. As they drift to sleep, Cypress jumps up, letting out a low growl. Julia pulls him close to her to quiet him, but he pushes away. Carmen sits up to pat Cypress' head. He pulls back, realizing the glow coming from his flared nostrils. Carmen and Julia frantically look around but can't see anything.

"Who's there? Show your face. I know you're there." Julia yells into the woods.

There is a rustle in the bushes behind them. Carmen twists around with fireballs ready in hand. Cypress crouches between them, growling at the bushes, puffs of smoke escaping his nostrils with each breath. Two men jump out of the bushes, landing in front of them. They crouch down in a poorly formed fighting stance. They look identical; maybe they're twins. They have short brown hair shaped into mohawks. Their eyes glow red. They are wearing tight red and black warrior-style suits. One has a thick stick in his hand with a snake carved down its shaft, the head at the top has a large red crystal in its mouth. The other has nothing but glowing red hands, looking ready to attack.

"I am Felix, and t-t-this is my broth-th-ther Keado. O-o-our m-m-master sent us here to-to-to kill you. We would like i-i-it if you d-d-don't fight b-b-back and just die in p-p-peace." The man with the stick, Felix, speaks with a deep, authoritative voice despite the stutter dragging out his command. Carmen and Julia look at each other and then at Felix and Keado.

"You think we're going to sit back and let you kill us? What kind of morons do you take us for?" Julia lets out a slight laugh as she rolls her eyes. Her shoulders relax slightly as she clears her throat. Carmen is tense and ready. *"Who is your master, and why do they want us dead?"*

Felix rolls his eyes at her. *"She wants r-r-r-revenge for w-w-what you've done. She doesn't c-c-care to see you a-a-alive."* Felix taps his staff to the ground, and the gem glows red. Julia squats down, fist at the ready. Cypress continues with a low growl as smoke puffs out his nostrils.

"Well, th-th-then you'll h-h-have to k-k-kill us." Julia mocks him.

His eyes narrow with anger. *"Th-th-then we will ta-ta-take you by f-f-force."*

Julia inhales deeply. Keado thrust a hand forward at them, sending a bright red lightning bolt through the air. Simultaneously, Carmen and Cypress shoot fireballs at the men, and Julia lets out a sonic scream. The scream amplifies the fireballs, expanding them and pushing them faster at the men. Keado is sent flying into a tree while Felix spins his staff,

creating a forcefield of red light that blocks
Julia's fiery scream. Keado jumps up, flinging
his hands repeatedly, sending red bolts at Julia.
One of the bolts hits her side, sending her to
the ground. Felix throws his staff at Carmen.
Carmen quickly waves his hand to the side,
creating a gust of air that sends it flying to
Keado. The staff penetrates through Keado's
stomach. Felix lets out a horrified scream.

Keado stands still as his arms fall to his
side. Blood slowly trickles from his mouth. He
looks down to see the impalement. Carmen and
Julia watch in silence. Still between Carmen
and Julia, Cypress bows his head with a
whimper. Keado places his hand on the staff
sticking out of him. His fingers weakly wrap
around it. His eyes flutter as his knees buckle.
Felix rushes over to him, putting a hand on his
back and neck and guiding him to the ground.
The stick sways back and forth as Keado
chokes, trying to breathe through the blood.
With one final gasp of breath, he goes limp, his
face pale and lips blue. He looks like he's aging

and withering away in seconds, right before their eyes. There is a long silence as they watch his cold, lifeless body become surrounded by blood. His brother is by his side crying. Julia begins to cry at what happened. She walks over to the two men on the ground, placing a hand on Keados lifeless body.

"G-g-get aw-w-w-way f-f-from usssss!" Felix stutters through his tears. Julia grabs his hands and pushes them off Keado. She moves slowly, ignoring his plea. Carmen and Cypress watch with confusion and worry Julia will get attacked. She pulls the staff from Keado's body and places her hand over the wound. Closing her eyes, her hair shifts as the wind picks up. Leaves cyclone around them, and thunder booms in the sky above the treetops. A white glow shines under her hands, and red tears stream down her cheeks. Carmen lunges forward; she doesn't seem to be breathing. Felix grabs his staff and backs away slowly. He smugly smiles as if this is what they wanted to happen. Cypress crouches down, huffing again, ready for Felix to attack. Carmen touches Julia's shoulders, and she falls limp in his arms. The wind stops blowing, and leaves flutter around as they fall to the ground. Her hands slide off Keado's stomach, and everyone gasps. Keado's wound is gone, and his stomach moves with shallow breaths. Felix whirls his staff above his head, chanting something Carmen can't hear. Cypress launches a fireball at him. Before the fireball can reach him, Felix lowers the staff, touching it to Keado's body, and the two men vanish.

Carmen lays Julia on a blanket. As her head touches the ground, she startles awake. Breathing heavily and looking around frantically, Carmen tries to calm her. Cypress runs over, laying his head in her lap for support. Carmen holds her head to his chest and takes steady breaths to help her calm. As her breathing calms, he describes to her everything that happened. Julia can only remember up until the staff pierced Keado. She has no idea what she has done, let alone how she has done it. Weak and tired, Carmen urges her to rest for the night, and he positions a towel under her head for a pillow. Julia drifts to sleep quickly as Carmen stays awake to stand watch for the night. They need to be sure nothing is coming back for them.

As the night progresses, Carmen drifts to sleep with the lulls of Cypress' snoring. Julia is awoken by the weight of Carmen's torso pushing down on her as he drifts deeper into sleep. As she rubs her eyes, she notices a small light off in the distance. She sits up to see what it is. It sways slowly with a walking bounce. The light illuminates the surrounding trees as it approaches. Julia gently shakes Carmen's shoulder. He sits up groggily. She points off into the distance, showing him the light. Not wanting to make a sound, she waves her hands around as if to ask what that is.

"I'm not sure. Hopefully, it's not the brothers with more friends." Carmen says in a low, soft voice. He grabs Julia around the waist, pulling her closer to him. Cypress continues snoring

away as if nothing is happening. As the light grows closer, the figure of a woman appears. As she ventures closer the blue light reveals her features. She appears older, her white hair is pulled back with a dark green bandana. Her eyes are bright emerald green radiating from her caramel skin. She holds a welcoming smile as her bouncing steps carry her closer to Carmen and Julia. They stare at her, mesmerized by her beauty.

"Hello, Julia and Carmen. You two look so cute together." The woman pulls her hand from the torch, floating it at her side. She claps her hands together, riding up on her toes with excitement. Cypress jolts awake at the clap of her hands. Julia pulls him in close to her to keep him calm.

"Cypress, my dear, you're still so small! But your bravery is greater than you know!" She leans in to pet him on his head.

"Do we know you?" Julia's voice is stern, filled with concern and confusion. The woman pulls back with a slight frown and a small gasp as she puts a hand to her mouth.

"Where are my manners? Y'all must think I'm some crazy old hag just bouncing around the woods. I am Illiana. You keep appearing in my crystal ball, and I've seen you face a few problems. I've been having signs pushing me to you. I have a feeling y'all will require my assistance on your journey. I can't deny destiny now, can I?" Illiana gives them a wink, followed by a big smile.

"Well, it's nice to meet you, Illiana," Julia jumps up to shake her hand.

Carmen smiles but hesitates to move forward. Carmen's uncle Menius had always taught him crystal balls can only be used to look for specific things. *Why was she looking for them?* He shakes his head and reaches a hand out to not be rude. Illiana reaches out, pulling them into a big hug. Carmen and Julia awkwardly hug her back. Until now, new people have been nothing but trouble for them. Still, something about Illiana seems trustworthy.

Illiana sits by the fire to tell them about her crystal ball, her take on how destiny works, and how she plans on helping them. Once she's done with her story, Carmen and Julia show her all the obstacles and stops left of their journey. The next stop is the swamp. Julia explains how they can cross it, but Illiana stops her mid-sentence.

"We need to stay here another day. You need to learn more about your powers, and I won't be with you for long. My end of the road will come, and I must depart. I am here to help you as best I can. The only way to do that is to stay here longer."

Carmen and Julia look at each other for a moment. They can see the pain in her eyes and the harshness in her tone. Hesitantly, they nod in agreement. Julia smiles, excited to learn more about her powers. Carmen is already in enough trouble. Another day to get home won't really matter at this point, especially if that means being more prepared for the journey ahead.

"Illiana, where would you like to sleep?" Carmen asks, pointing to his and Julia's makeshift beds. Illiana flashes a smile and gets up, walking over to a thick patch of trees. She firmly plants her feet on the ground and begins waving her hands from side to side. The trees start rattling and swaying. She twists her ankles to face her feet outward, and the trees start twisting and bending before their eyes. Soon, a little hut forms out of the newly shaped trees. She begins quietly whispering words, unheard by Carmen and Julia, and the hut glows a bright yellow. She blows a kiss at it, sending a shock wave out, causing leaves to scatter all over and everyone to cover their faces. She grabs her floating torch and heads into the hut. She pulls back the small door of bark that formed during the hut's creation. She waves them good night as she crawls into the hut and shuts the door behind her. Carmen and Julia stand still, speechless. There are small gaps in the logs and sticks, but they can't see the torch's light or Illiana's movements from within. Carmen grabs his blanket and sits by

the fire. Julia lays against his shoulder and pulls her blanket around her as well. Carmen puts his arm around her as they fall asleep in each other's arms.

When they wake in the morning, Carmen and Cypress set off to get some sticks to maintain the fire for the day and set some traps. Illiana takes Julia to the riverside to train on her powers. First, they start with air and then transition to water. Next, they work with static and levitation. Julia is amazed at how each power leads into the next and how easily she's able to pick it up. It helps that Illiana has similar powers, and she is such a great teacher. She feels terrible that Carmen has been struggling to help her learn, but she knows he is still learning how his powers work. Illiana wants to work on Julia's healing abilities to wrap up training. They had told her what happened with Felix and Keado. Illiana has Julia focus on the back of her hand. With a quick swipe of her sharp fingernail, Illiana cuts the back of Julia's hand. Julia let out a shriek, pulling her hand to her chest. She takes a deep breath and exhales slowly. A single tear forms in the corner of her eye and drips onto her hand. Slowly waving her hand over the cut, it begins to glow. She can feel the energy pushing against the wound as the blood slowly recedes back into the open wound and closes up. Julia and Illiana jump with joy.

Back at the camp, Carmen has already started making lunch. Julia sits by the fire, looking at the photo of her parents. She wishes they could see her today and how powerful she has become. They would be so proud of her.

"My dear, you must learn to let go of the past and live in the future. It's okay to remember them, but you can't dwell." Illiana takes Julia's hand in hers. "The more you let go, the stronger you will become."

A tear falls from Julia's eye, landing on the picture. She looks at it for a moment. "They're my parents. They were all I had, and someone else took them from me. I can't let go of that." Julia wipes her eyes as Illiana takes

the picture from her hand. Carmen notices
Illiana raising her hand with the picture before
it slips from her hand and drops to the ground.
Julia quickly crouches to the ground to pick up
the shattered pieces of the frame.

"You need to let them go." Illiana's voice is
harsh. Julia snaps her head up, shooting an
angry glare at Illiana. "What I mean, my dear,
is it's sad they are gone, and it's okay to be sad.
But you have so much more now. You have
Carmen, Cypress, and myself. You have powers
that are a wonderful gift from your mother, so
in a way, she is still with you." Illiana's voice
softens, becoming kinder.

Julia looks at the picture, a tear slipping
from her eye. She carefully folds the picture
and places it in her shirt to keep it close.
Illiana picks up the glass and wooden frame
and tosses them into the fire so no one steps
on them.

"I know what I have, and I am grateful
for it. I am beyond excited for the future,
especially now that I have Carmen and

Cypress." Julia pauses for a moment, looking at Carmen. She hasn't forgotten he unexpectedly asked her to come with him when they had the portal map. Her whole being is scared to say yes; this is her home, the only place she's ever known. But she wants to scream yes with every fiber of her being. She just hasn't figured out how to address it. Carmen smiles warmly at her, his eyes glistening from the fire. *"But I can still be sad about the past when I don't know what happened or why. I still need some sort of closure."*

Illiana reaches out and grabs Julia's hand. Julia looks at Illiana; her smile fades as she pleads silently with her. *"My dear, you are entitled to closure but can't let finding it be your weakness. I have been watching you closely through my crystal ball, and you fall weak when answers are possibly at your grasp. I can tell you now that the witch from the cave is not dead."*

Julia gasps, pulling her hand back to cover her mouth.

"She is weak and healing, but she will be back, and I just want you to be ready, my dear. The two men that attacked you last night were sent by her."

Julia lunges forward, hugging Illiana. Carmen watches skeptically as he spoons some stew into bowls. Something is off about Illiana, but he has no idea what or why. She is kind and gentle but also strong. She has all the answers and knows exactly what to do. *How could she know all this from a crystal ball unless she was looking for it intentionally?* She is hiding something, *but what?* Carmen looks at Julia's smiling face; she seems happy and comfortable with Illiana. He shrugs it off, wanting to trust Julia's instinct. Carmen hands everyone a bowl of stew and sits by the fire. Cypress lies beside him, falling fast asleep for his afternoon nap.

As they eat, Julia is talking to Carmen about her training and how well she is doing. Carmen listens intently as Julia's excitement about her powers increases. Illiana sits listening happily

174

at first, then Carmen notices her drifting off into her thoughts. He is trying to be happy about Illianas's sudden appearance, but something is telling him there's more to her story.

"Is everything okay, Illiana?" Carmen asks during a break in Julia's excitement. Illiana shoots a quick, panicking glance up at him. She shakes her head and takes a quick breath.

"Everything is fine, dear. Why do you ask?" She gives Carmen a half smile. Julia turns to her worried. Illiana places a hand on her shoulder, holding her half smile. "Really, dears, everything is fine. There is nothing to worry about. I'm just relaxing, listening to how excited you are about your powers."

Julia smiles and lays back to look at the sky through the trees. Carmen still isn't convinced.

"Well, you look a little worried or something," Carmen says in disbelief. Illiana doesn't speak for a moment; she stares blankly at Carmen. Slowly, she stands up and heads for her hut. At the door, she pauses, turning back to see Carmen and Julia intently watching her, waiting for an answer.

"Dears, I am perfectly fine. There is no need to worry about me. I just need to rest for a bit, and we can get back to training."

Carmen shakes his head, rolling his eyes to the side. He lays back, brushing his hand over Cypress. Illiana ducks into the hut's opening, pulling the bark door shut behind her. Julia shoots a look of annoyance at Carmen.

"Why would you put her on the spot like that? Don't pressure her and scare her off. She is here to help us when she doesn't have to." Julia jumps up, hand on her hip and finger wagging at him. Carmen chuckles slightly as he rolls to his side to see her better.

"I'm not trying to scare her off. You don't think it's odd with her timing; how does she know so much from a crystal ball? How does she know so much about your powers? I just have a weird feeling. I'm being cautious, that's *all. I feel like there is something more she's not telling us."*

Julia rolls her eyes and storms off. Carmen throws up his hands in frustration and heads to the river for some water. Cypress follows behind him. Julia wanders over to Illiana's hut and knocks on the door. Illiana opens the door and looks at Julia with saddened eyes.

"Illiana, there's something wrong. You can tell me if you want." She can feel a strange energy coming off Illiana. She looks sad, but the energy feels like frustration. She catches herself thinking maybe Carmen is right for a moment, but she brushes it off quickly. Illiana is sweet, kind, and gentle. There is nothing weird about her.

"Yes, I know. I don't want to worry you or anything, my dear." Illiana wipes a tear from her cheek and gives Julia a small smile.

"You're not going to worry me, I promise,"

Illiana steps out and shuts the door behind her. They walk over to the fire and sit down together. She looks up at Julia and lets out a little sigh.

"Okay, I will tell you. But you can't tell Carmen. I know he is skeptical about my presence, and this would make him distrust me more." Illiana pauses and waits for a moment.

Julia looks at her, confused, and suspiciously, she nods in agreement. "I should start with the fact that I haven't been frank with you." Illiana's words are soft as she speaks. Her eyes are hard and focused. Julia begins to tear up. She has the oddest feeling, Carmen's gut feeling is right, but she doesn't want to break Illiana's trust.

"How so?" Julia lets out a little gasp, covering her mouth. She gives Illiana her complete attention.

"The evil witch that has been attacking you is my sister Magnis. I know she is still alive because I can still feel her energy. I can tell she is weak, but she is growing stronger."

Julia covers her mouth as her hand trembles. She can feel her anger growing. She jumps up, backing away slowly. *"She's your sister! So you're just here to take my powers from me, aren't you!"* Julia can feel herself yelling, but she doesn't care. Illiana looks around frantically as she puts a finger over her lips to hush her.

"No, no, you have it all wrong, my dear. We are from two different covens. I have my own powers that differ from yours, and if they were to mix, it would be deadly for me and everyone around me. I am here to protect you from her. I haven't spoken to her in years, and I heard she and her coven got into trouble with one of their own, but I had no idea how bad it was until recently."

Julia takes a deep breath as she lowers herself back to the ground.

"I have been having visions of her killing you and Carmen, and I can't let that happen. In my most recent vision, she kills all of us, including me. She has already killed the rest of her coven and harnessed what's left of their

powers to ensure she can match yours. She may not look like much, but she is fast and smart. How else do you think she survived the collapse of the caves."

Julia stares at Illiana with wide eyes and confusion. So many emotions and thoughts run through her head. *Is she lying? Is Carmen right to be worried? Is she telling the truth? Are they all about to die?* "How can we beat her, then? We need a plan. Do you know where she finds us? We need to be ready; we need to tell Carmen so he can be ready!" Julia starts breathing heavily as panic setting in. Illiana quickly crawls over to her, hugging her. Julia pulls back angrily, pushing Illiana back slightly. "Wait! How can you be so calm?" Illiana gasps at Julia's aggression. There is a long pause before Illiana speaks.

"My dear, I am calm because I know the great power that you and Carmen possess. Carmen is capable of things beyond imagination. He just doesn't know it yet. My visions scare me, but they can change." Illiana's emerald eyes twinkle from the firelight.

Julia softens her gaze a bit but looks more confused now. She has no idea what to believe or think. *Is Illiana lying? Does she have an ulterior motive? Is she genuinely trying to help them?* She wants to believe Carmen's feelings are right, but something deep in her gut wants her to trust and believe Illiana. She gives in and smiles at Illiana before pulling her in for a hug.

Illiana lets out a big sigh of relief. *"My dear, please promise me one thing."* She leans back and holds Julia's shoulders in her hands. *"Carmen must not know Magnis is my sister. He already doesn't trust me, and I am afraid this will push him away even more. We need his trust if we are going to defeat her."*

Julia thinks for a moment; it's bad enough she's choosing to trust Illiana despite Carmen's skepticism. To withhold this information feels wrong. She doesn't want to lie to him and pretend his concerns aren't valid. However, Illiana is right; they will need Carmen's trust if they want to defeat Magnis. Even though lying to Carmen may break his trust, Julia nods in agreement.

"Thank you, my dear. I just want what's best for you and Carmen. I promise he will find out in time, but when he is ready."

Julia continues nodding.

In It Together

J ulia and Illiana decide to head for the river to meet up with Carmen and Cypress. Illiana suggests now would be a good time for more training. They walk in silence, Julia is still struggling with her agreement to keep Illiana's secret. She hates the thought of keeping something from Carmen. He is the first person in her life she has truly trusted and relied on and now she feels like she's going to let him down. She cares a lot about Carmen, perhaps she even loves Carmen? Her heart pounds at the idea of deceiving a loved one. Will he hate her when he finds out? Will he still want her to go home with him? She takes slow deep breaths. She hasn't had the courage to ask him if he was serious about his offer to take her and Cypress with him. The thought scared her at first. The reality that she almost left her universe, her home so quickly, without a second thought is terrifying. But, it makes her happy to think about going somewhere she can live a happier life, a life with Carmen. She smiles at the idea, then frowns again remembering she is going to have to keep Illiana's secret. Julia looks over at Illiana who seems to be walking with a happy bounce. Her hands brush against every tree she passed so that she can feel the energy within. Slowly Julia reaches out to do the same. She touches a passing tree, then another, and another. She tries distracting herself from her own torturous thoughts.

Off in the distance she hears splashing. Carmen is laughing as Cypress squeaks and squeals. She smiles big and starts running for the water. Illiana laughs as she picks up running after her. At the edge of the water Julia and Illiana come to a dead stop. Their eyes are wide with shock. Cypress flies over the water swirling in circles. In front of him moves a giant orb of water. They look at Carmen who is clapping and laughing as he cheers on

Cypress. Carmen smiles when he notices them standing by the river.

"Look, he has water powers too!" Carmen shouts trying to overpower Cypress' squeals. Illiana covers her mouth as Julia whistles loudly to Cypress. Carmen covers his ears. Cypress turns to look at her causing him to lose focus and crash into the river. "What's wrong, he's just having fun?" Carmen looks at Illiana and Julia confused. He can see the horrified looks on their faces. He doesn't know much about dragons but is excited to watch him learn new powers.

"DO NOT DO THAT AGAIN!" Julia yells shouting at the two of them. "No one can see him do this! Dragons only have one ability. Dragons with multiple abilities get hunted and killed. They are unaffected by the curses making them uncontrollable and able to break the rules and treaties in place. If anyone finds out they will kill him!" Julia shouts as she looks around in a panic.

Illiana places a hand on Julia's shoulder. Julia takes a deep breath and reaches down to place a hand on Cypress' chin. He crawls to her feet, ears folded back in fear, scared of her shouting.

"I love you, my sweet baby boy. No one will ever harm you if it's the last thing I do." Julia looks into Cypress' eyes as she strokes the side of his face. He closes his eyes and rubs his head into her hand.

Carmen steps out of the water and over to Cypress and Julia. He crouches down, hunching over Cypress to hug him. "I will protect you at all costs."

Cypress rolls onto his back with another whimper. Carmen rubs his hand over his belly. There is no longer fur on his belly; in its place are long, smooth scales. They are hard like a shell but still move and flex with each breath.

Illiana clears her throat, breaking the silence. "My dears, it seems we have some more training to do, that includes you Cypress. You'll

need to learn control so you don't get caught."
Carmen and Julia give Illiana a smile. Julia
places her head against Cypress letting out a
sigh. Carmen mouths the words thank you to
Illiana. She flashes a smile as she nods her
head. Illiana lets them relish in the moment for
a bit before clapping at them to get up to start
training. They spend the rest of the day
training and goofing off. Even Illiana gets in on
the fun by throwing water balls at them while
hiding behind a tree. Cypress flies around and
sprays her with water from behind.

As the sun begins to set they head back to
camp for some dinner. Illiana cooks up a
vegetable medley with some fish Cypress pulled
from the river. Cypress eats his food quickly
and then proceeds to pass out between Carmen
and Julia. They laugh as he snores and twitches
in his sleep. Illiana takes her food and heads to
bed in her hut, leaving Carmen and Julia on
their own. They sit and talk for hours until Julia
drifts to sleep. Carmen stays up watching the

flames die down before drifting off to sleep himself.

In the morning Carmen awakes to Julia hugging his arm. He smiles at her, admiring her soft gentle face. A small chunk of her red hair drapes over her cheek. He pulls it back slowly to wake her. There is a loud thud and the ground rumbles. Julia jolts awake pushing back on Carmen. His head hits the ground as he rolls to get up. Illiana strolls out from a group of trees. She has a warm smile on her face as she approaches Julia.

"Good morning, my dears. I'm glad to see you're finally awake. Cypress just went to get some firewood. Carmen, can you stay here and wait for him? Julia and I are going to do some more training. I should warn you that Cypress went through a bit of a growth spurt last night. Be careful." She gives a wink to Carmen as she grabs Julia's hand, pulling her into the woods. Carmen gives a sheepish wave to Julia as she's whisked away.

"How long will you be gone?" Carmen yells as Illiana walks away quickly, almost running, dragging Julia behind her. Julia gives Carmen a quick wave as she stumbles trying to keep up with Illiana. Illiana seems extra excited about today's training.

"Only an hour's time my dear, we won't be long. I know we need to get going today." Carmen keeps watching until they're out of sight. He thinks for a moment. *What did she mean? Cypress had a growth spurt?* He shrugs it off as he decides to pack things up. He is almost finished packing when he hears a loud thud. It's the same thud that woke Julia this morning. He snaps his head in the direction of the noise. Slowly he wanders that way keeping low to the ground. He follows the sound ducking behind trees to keep hidden. As he travels further down the path he can hear scraping sounds. As the scraping gets closer Carmen feels himself lose the direction of the sound. It sounds like he is right on top of it but he can't see anything. He stops for a moment trying to focus on the sound. He leans forward around a large tree putting his weight on a small branch. Seeing nothing he pushes on the branch to push himself back up when the branch snaps sending him spiraling to the ground. Laying on his back Carmen catches a glimpse of something large falling at his face. Quickly he recoils, covering his face. Carmen feels something large on both sides of him. There are loud swooshing and flapping sounds with big gusts of wind. Scared, Carmen slowly peaks through his hands not wanting to see how he dies. He is greeted with a large dragon head in his face. There's a loud squeal as Carmen's face gets assaulted with a large tongue. He pushes back against the dragon's face trying to slide his body out to stand up.

"Cypress is that you! How have you grown this big overnight?" Carmen yells with excitement. Cypress lets out a quick squeal as he prances around like a puppy. Cypress has grown taller than Carmen's height and his wingspan is longer than his body. On the tops of each wing are white points that match the horns on top of his head. He no longer has any fur, just scales of all different colors of metallic shimmer. His claws are long, black, and riddled with wood splinters. This must have been the scraping sound he had been following. Looking up at the trees he can see they are missing big chunks. There are chewed-up logs perfect for a fire all over the ground. Cypress smiles big, showing more wood splinters between his teeth. Carmen smiles rubbing Cypress' head as he pushes it against him. Carmen turns slightly to his side trying not to get impaled with his new horns. "You're a good boy buddy. Let's get this wood back to camp so we can figure out how to take it with us." Cypress lets out a screech and bolts off into the woods. Carmen shakes his head laughing as he picks up the logs. Moments later Cypress trots back with a large wagon strolling behind him. There is a thick rope that loops around his neck attaching to each side of the wagon. "Where did yo-, You know what I don't care let's load this bad boy up." Cypress and Carmen scoop up all the wood, tossing it into the wagon. Once back at camp, Carmen fixes the wood so that it's neater, allowing them room to fit the rest of their belongings with room to spare.

~Julia and Illiana~

"Okay dear do you see the movement in the bark and feel the life of the tree?" Illiana stands in front of a tree and slowly sways it back and forth to let Julia feel the energy between herself and the tree. "Okay one more time," Illiana says, placing Julia in front of the tree she was moving. Julia places her hand on the tree and closes her eyes. The tree shakes and moves, then the tree shrinks down to the size of Julia. Frustrated, Julia clenches her hands into a fist, pulling back to punch the tree. Illiana grabs her fist and gently puts her hand to her side. "You need to relax my dear. You'll get this in time. It's not easy deary."

"I don't get what I am doing wrong. I feel the energy and I bend it how I want to, yet it's

192

not doing what I want." Julia says exasperated, trying to take deep breaths to relax.

"Dear as I've told you before, powers grow and develop with practice. You will get it in time." Illiana reminds her, turning Julia to face her. She places her hands on Julia's shoulders and looks deep into her eyes. Julia takes a deep breath and gives her a small smile. Illiana lights a ball of light and holds it out to Julia. Slowly she reaches out and takes the ball of light. She looks intently as she moves her free hand around it. The ball begins to shrink and grow with the movement of her hand. She slowly pulls her hands apart making the ball grow larger. She turns her hands facing away from her and gives a hard push. The ball of light flies forward hitting a tree. Bark scatters everywhere with the explosion. Julia closes her eyes with a big smile as she takes in this moment.

"See my dear, it took you over two hours to learn how to move just a small bit of energy yet

you got it with practice. You will get this too, just keep trying."

Julia nods, rolling her eyes in defeat. Illiana is right, she can't let herself feel defeated while learning. She wants to be part of the team, be able to help out when situations get bad, and play fire toss with Carmen and Cypress. Julia sighs as she continues behind Illiana to camp.

When they get back to camp they can't find Carmen or Cypress. Both of them stay silent for a moment. Everything's gone except the remaining embering fire which has been recently snuffed out with water. Julia screams out their names hoping for a response. She calls out once more as she hears a rustle in the bushes.

"Very funny guys come on out now we need to get going." Julia waits but the only response is more rustling from the trees. Julia walks over slowly to expose them.

Four Witches Clan

Suddenly, Magnis and the twins jump out from the bushes. Keado shoots a green bolt of energy, tying Illiana and Julia to a tree. Julia screams as Magnis hurries over to cover her mouth. Julia bites down on her hand, turning her head away in disgust as Magnis pulls her hand back to inspect it.

"You wretched child, is that any way to treat your grandmother?" Magnis cackles. "Illiana, my dear sister, I see you haven't got what you wanted yet." She gives her a wink while still laughing. She grabs Julia's chin and pulls her face forward to look into her eyes. Julia pulls back, spitting in her eye. Magnis lets out an eeeek as she wipes her eye.

"Leave us alone, you nasty bitch! I thought we established you aren't my grandmother. It was just another lie you told me to get close." Julia scowls at her, wiggling back and forth to break free. Magnis clenches her fist in anger, punching Julia in the stomach. Julia's body tenses in pain as all the air pushes out of her lungs.

"Why does everything have to be so dramatic with you, Magnis? Just take what you want and leave people alone. She has no part in what happened." Illiana's voice is calm and sweet. Julia snaps her head up at her, scowling. Julia isn't about to give up her powers without a fight.

"Take what I want, you say? What about what you want, dear sister?" Magnis' tone is mocking. Julia looks back and forth between the two, confused. Illiana scowls at her and then looks at Julia with sad eyes. There is silence for a moment, Julia waits for someone to fill her in on the information only they seem to know. "It seems like you haven't been honest with Julia, so I will help you settle and make your choice." Magnis takes a white powder from her pocket and blows it into their faces.

They cough, choking on the powder before passing out.

"A-A-Are you going to k-k-kill them now, m-m-mama?" Felix asks, jumping up and down in excitement. Keado, slow in reaction, catches on and begins clapping while jumping up and down.

Magnis storms over, smacking them both in the back of the head.

"No, you stuttering idiot. Not yet; I want them to suffer. Take them to the cave and lock them away before they wake up."

Keado pulls back his power, untying them from the tree. Their limp, unconscious bodies fall to the ground. Magnis kicks Illiana and Julia as she walks by. She clenches her hand into a fist, thrusting a small fireball at Illiana's hut, catching the hut on fire.

"I've always hated her precious huts. Once I regain my strength, I'll never have to see them again." Magnis sighs and storms off into the woods. Felix picks up Julia and follows her. Keado struggles to lift Illiana onto his shoulder for a second before tailing off behind the others.

Julia awakes to a small blade poking at the side of her face. She jumps, and the blade makes a small cut in the corner of her cheek. *"Where is Illiana and Carmen?"* Julia says, still feeling a little drowsy. Blood drips down to the corner of her mouth. Her head rolls back and forth as she tries to focus her eyes to see where she is. A hand steadies her head as her eyes focus enough to see who is in front of her.

"I killed them and made their skin into blankets for my bed," Magnis says, laughing maniacally. She gently runs the knife down Julia's face, picking up some of the blood. She sticks her tongue out, licking it off the knife. *"MMMM, I can taste and feel my power. Soon,*

I'll have them back." Julia shutters, trying to pull back. She can't move her arms or legs; she realizes she's tied up with a thick rope. She wiggles to break free, but the ropes only get tighter. She tries to yell, but nothing comes out. Her throat burns and scratches as if she's been crying for hours. Magnis laughs while patting Julia's head. *"Calm down, they're fine for now. I will let them live but under one condition. You must replace your mother's position in the four Witches Clan and help us unleash a powerful spell that will release the dragons from the curse tying them to Dragon Forest. What do you say?"* Magnis looks into Julia's eyes. Julia looks like she is trying to pull her head free.

"You're insane!" She gives her legs another kick to try and break them free, but the restraints don't budge. Magnis laughs again.

"Just think your friend can leave this place and go home safe, sound, and happy... You can have unlimited power." Magnis laughs again, raising her hands to the air, letting tiny sparks of power flow from her fingers like static. Julia

sighs as she hangs her head. Her eyes close as she focuses on steadying her breathing.

"Fine, I will help you, as long as Illiana, Carmen, and Cypress aren't harmed, and you let them go so Carmen can go home!" Julia sighs, hoping to convince Magnis, buying her time to devise a plan to get away. She hopes Carmen and Illiana will go without fighting too much, having to leave her behind.

"Wow, that was quick. I thought it'd take more convincing. I guess you're not as stupid as you seem." Magnis pulls a small black rock out of her pocket and holds it to her mouth. She speaks softly into it. *"She agreed; meet me here at midnight."* Magnis spins the rock in her fingers, and it vanishes, leaving a small cloud of smoke.

"Let me see them, I want to know where they are! Are they okay? Let them go!" Julia yells, getting agitated.

"Not so fast. We don't have much time. I need to teach you about the four Witches' Clan. You must learn to harness the magic of the clan to cast the spell," Magnis says, impatiently pacing the floors with an agitated look.

"If it's the four witches' Clan, who are the other two witches?" Julia says, trying to sound interested. She needs to keep up a ruse to get what she wants. Magnis stops pacing and looks at her, seeming annoyed by her questions.

"I guess if you're going to help us, you'll need to know. The other two are Felix and Keado. Your healing of Keado was just the beginning of our bond. It is precisely what we needed to start all this."

Julia's eyes widen with the sound of their names.

Magnis continues pacing, growing more agitated. "My people found them abandoned in the woods. Felix had his name written on his blanket, but Keado didn't. I gave him that name

201

after my father when I took them in. As
members of the clan died, they transferred
their powers to Keado and Felix to carry on the
Clan. They could be so much stronger, but you
have a great deal of our shared power. Once
you join the clan, we will all share the power
equally."

Julia's heart sinks. Magnis has a kind side
to her. She can't help but understand her
perspective. She goes to speak, but Magnis
continues to tell her story.

"When I was fifteen, I was shunned from my
tribe because I didn't look like everyone else. I
was born pale and sickly looking while
everyone else shared their beautiful smooth
caramel skin. My body lacks pigment and I
can't spend time in the sun. As a child, I was
unable to help with farming or washing in the
stream. The village believed I was cursed at
birth and my life would be their demise. They
banished me from the village. While looking for
a safe place to sleep I stumbled upon the
Witches' Den Cave. Inside the cold damp cave
were these sweet ladies who took me in and
accepted me as their own. They used their

powers to bring good to the people and get food for us. People praised us for all the good we did. When your mother left, we weren't as strong. She broke her connection, leaving us with fewer powers to share. The strength of our powers comes from the four elements. The northern air, southern fire, east earth, and western waters. People started looking down upon us when we weren't strong enough to bring them everything we had before."

Julia sees a tear run down Magnis' face. She realizes Magnis just wants to be loved and accepted.

"So what is it, and how does it work?" Julia tries to feign interest. She wants to change the subject; she doesn't want to think of her parents. "I am so sorry for what happened to you. You have a heart of gold, and you deserve so much better, regardless of your powers." Julia speaks with a softer tone, genuinely interested in learning more. She wants to know how Illiana plays into this. "Why are we going to take over Dragon Forest?"

Magnis stops pacing the floor and looks into Julia's eyes briefly studying her face to see if she's genuinely interested. "Dragon Forest was my people's land. If I can get it back for them, I will earn their trust back, and they will welcome me back... My people and the dragons once lived in peace, sharing the land and resources together. When the curse was placed that dragons could no longer hunt off the land, food ran short, the dragons turned on my people, driving them away, and they've struggled ever since." Magnis turns her attention away from Julia.

There's something she can hear that Julia can't. Julia stretches her neck to look around, but the woods are dark. There's only a small lantern hanging from a low tree branch. "That's enough talk for now. It's time. Tie them to the tree and get in a circle." Magnis' command is directed to someone Julia can't see.

Magnis flicks her wrist, torches around the forest light up. The twins tie Carmen and Illiana

204

to a tree. Their mouths are wrapped shut with cloth. The twins join Magnis on a circle drawn in the dirt in the center of the forest opening. Julia can hear Carmen trying to yell at her as he wiggles, trying to break free. Illiana stands motionless as tears trickle down her face. She can see a blue glow around Carmen and Illiana's wrists. *That must be why they haven't used their powers to break free.* Her attention is caught by another flick of Magnis' wrists. The ropes binding Julia loosen. Julia frantically brushes the ropes off as she rises to her feet. A squeaking noise catches her attention on Carmen's side. Cypress walks over his wings and front paws bound with the same blue, glowing rope as Carmen and Illiana. There is rope tying his mouth shut and a wagon full of their stuff behind him. He lets out a small whimper as he looks at Julia with sad eyes. She's caught off guard by how much he's grown. She hadn't seen him before Magnis, and the twins ambushed her.

Magnis clears her throat and points at the ground beside her, indicating she wants Julia to join the circle. Felix and Keado close their eyes and stretch their arms out, palms facing up. They start glowing green and rise into the air; Magnis follows behind them. They hover there with glowing hands stretched to each other, barely out of reach. Magnis slowly reaches her hand down to Julia.

"Just step into the circle, and it will lift you into the air. Feel the breeze surrounding you. I'll do the rest." Julia hesitates for a moment before reaching out and grabbing Magnis' hand. Julia starts glowing green and rises with the others. Carmen wiggles aggressively, trying to break free. The cloth falls from his mouth as he screams for Julia to stop. Magnis begins chanting some words, and the two boys join in. Julia yells in pain as she feels her powers start seeping out of her and flow into the others.

Julia gasps; she realizes she's being tricked. She tries to fight it and starts flailing around, struggling in the air. She can feel her body growing weak. She pulls her hand free from Magnis', The power transfer stops and all the power pushes back into Julia's body. She drops to the ground. The three reach out with both hands, using their powers they start trying to pull her back into the circle. Julia notices a big book in the middle and dives to grab it. As her fingers wrap around the book's edges, she begins to rise again. This time, she turns blue, and information from the book floods her mind. Her eyes widen as the information overwhelms her. Magnis grabs her wrist and shakes the book from her hands. Her blue glow fades, and the green light starts absorbing her again. Julia smiles wide as she begins to chant.

"I banish you by the powers of the goddess' and gods. I banish you by the powers of the sun, moon, and stars. I banish you by the powers of Earth, air, fire, and water."

Julia repeats the spell over and over. Their green glow flickers and fades as the spell repeats. Magnis and the twins drop to the ground. Julia points a finger at them.

"I BANISH YOU!" Julia yells as the twins turn to stone. Magnis cries out as she lunges for her boys. She waves her arm in a circle, creating a green glow. Julia flicks her finger once more. "I BANISH YOU!" There is a large puff of smoke. As the air clears, there is nothing but a pile of ash. Julia lowers to the ground and runs over to Carmen and Illiana. She puts her middle and index fingers together from each hand and pulls them apart hard. The bindings and the blue glow disintegrate into a cloud of ash. She turns to Cypress and repeats the same motion. Cypress lets out a loud squeal of excitement as he leaps high in the sky, stretching out his wings. Julia hurls her body at Carmen and Illiana, hugging them tight. Cypress drops hard to the ground; Julia leaps in for a hug as he wraps his neck around her. Carmen follows behind Illiana as she inspects the circle and book on the ground.

"I always hoped this day would come. I wasn't prepared for the disconnect I would feel now that she's gone. We have always been connected, I could always feel her presence, but now it's silent." Tears fall from Illiana's face as she wanders over to the pile of ashes where her sister had been. Carmen walks over and places a hand on her shoulder. He's upset that Illana is keeping such a big secret, but he still feels sorry for her. Julia grabs his hand and pulls him away from her. Although confused, Carmen follows her.

"Well, as you told me once, you need to let go to be strong. I know it's hard, but you don't get to be sad when I can't." Julia's tone is harsh and mocking. She bends down to pick up the spell book. "Put this in the wagon, please; we must set up camp. There is a cave just up the path." Julia hands the book back in Carmen's direction. He reaches out to grab it. As his fingers connect with the book, orange sparks shoot out, touching the book and Julia's hand. Carmen can feel anger and confusion coming from Julia. He brushes it off and places it carefully in the wagon. He doesn't want to upset her more, so he figures they can address it later. Illiana blows a kiss at the ashes before following down the path.

"My dear, is everything okay? You seem upset. You should be happy you defeated her." Illiana's voice is soft, still filled with sadness.

Julia doesn't answer at first. She walks quickly and steadily ahead of everyone. Her feelings are conflicted; she has no idea what to think or feel. She has no idea if Illiana is actually there to help them or if she has other intentions. After touching the book, she knows that most of Magnis' story is true. The book rebuilt the connection her mother once shared with the clan allowing her to share memories with each of them for a moment. It left her with more questions than answers. She's determined to find the answers and knows the book is her key to those answers.

"We have a lot to talk about, and I want the truth!" Julia's voice is harsh, and Illiana shutters as she knows exactly what Julia's referring to. "How could you let your family shun your sister for being different? It wasn't because she was evil or mistreating others." Julia stops hard and turns around to get into Illiana's tear filled face. Julia tries to remain strong but begins to cry. She wants to trust Illiana, but everything she has learned in the last few hours proves she can't.

"My dear, it's complicated, but I promise you will have the truth. She was the weakest in our village, and everyone believed her to be cursed, plaguing death upon our people. My parents didn't believe this; we all loved her. When the king cursed the dragons, he promised to also curse us to protect us, but we had to sacrifice my sister. My parents didn't want to give up their daughter, they said no and fought back. As food ran low for the dragons, they began picking us off one by one. To protect our people, my parents faked her death and banished her from the land. They hid her in Dracfalls to live out her life. When she found the Four witches Clan and shared their power, it drew the king's attention. He was not happy and wanted her dead. He turned the dragons against us, causing panic. I knew she would free the curse on the dragons to give our people their home. But she didn't know that our family wouldn't be welcomed back, including her. What my parents did shunned them from the village. The village moved underground to hide, While my parents were forced to leave Dragon Forest." Illiana wipes tears from her eyes as she waits for a response.

Julia is unmoved, still full of mixed emotions.

"My meeting you was not of ill intent but rather orders from higher up to stop her. It has pained me to feel and watch her struggle. I wanted nothing more than to be with her and help. I even came to her Joining the Four Witches Clan for a short time, begging her to rejoin the family once we were banished, but she rejected me removing me from the Clan, rightfully so. I was still heartbroken, we were just children when everything happened. Once removed from the clan I didn't have powers to *stop any of this from happening? I didn't get my powers until years later when my coven recruited me."*

Julia reaches out and places a hand on Illiana's shoulder. She looks at her with softer eyes as a tear rolls down her face. Julia pulls a hand from behind her back, showing Illiana that her hand is glowing blue. Illiana nods with understanding.

"I am sorry, thank you for telling me the truth." Julia blows on her hand, and the glowing fades away with the air like glitter falling from her hand. *"I've been lied to so many times I wanted to make sure I got the truth."*

Illiana gives her a slight smile. As she leans forward to hug her. *"My dear, I am so proud of your inner strength. It takes little energy to use a truth spell, but it takes immense strength to control your emotions while doing so."*

Julia smiles back as she presses her body into the hug.

"I promise I will tell you everything from now on. I won't let you question anything with me again. My dear, you are an extraordinary person, and you are destined for great things. I want to see you get there, which is the truth." Illiana leans back, looking at Carmen and Cypress. They both flash an awkward smile. Pretending they hadn't been listening the whole time. Carmen noticed Julia was up to something and trusted her to do what was needed.

At the cave, they quickly move to set up sleeping areas and a small fire for warmth. Everyone except Cypress agrees they aren't hungry, so he sets off on his own to do some hunting. Tucked into their blankets, Carmen and Illiana fall asleep faster than their heads could hit the bags they were using as a makeshift pillow. Julia lies awake, troubled by her new secret. Their fight isn't over yet.

All is Lost

When the sun rises, everyone works together to quickly load the wagon to start the day. Upon leaving the cave, Julia looks at the map to plan the safest path. Carmen walks behind Julia, mesmerized by her swaying hips. The shorts she's wearing are tighter than the ones she usually wears, highlighting her hourglass figure perfectly. Carmen is trying not to be disrespectful; she's the most beautiful person to him, inside and out. She picked the shorts out at the shop in Dracfalls. It was the one thing she wanted for herself.

Illiana and Cypress walk side by side, watching Carmen and Julia. Illiana makes taunting comments and kissy faces behind Carmen and Julia's backs, causing Cypress to laugh. Carmen and Julia look back in confusion, but Illiana and Cypress play it off by looking in different directions and whistling. The growing affection between them is so thick everyone around them can feel it.

After a few miles of walking in the awkwardness of Carmen's mesmerized gaze and Cypress and Illiana's taunting giggles, Julia comes to a dead stop, twists around and shoves the map at everyone.

"Well, since you all want to keep muttering between yourselves and giggling, maybe you can help me find a way through the swamp so we don't have to waste two days going around." Julia's tone is harsh and filled with annoyance. Everyone becomes quiet as they look at the ground. No one speaks until Julia clears her throat to motivate them.

"What's in the swamp that can kill us? Can we just swim through it?" Carmen speaks up quickly, not wanting to upset Julia more. Julia lowers her brows at him before remembering Carmen isn't from this universe.

"Well, it ha-."

"There are man-eating plants with thorny vines that will grab you and kill you. You can't even fly over it because there is a thick gas in the air that is toxic to breathe." Illiana replies, cutting Julia off mid-sentence.

"Maybe we can create a force field of air around us?" Carmen says, walking to Julia's side. He takes her hand, gently pulling her to slow her pace. "We can do it together; I know we can."

Julia rolls her eyes at him. "We don't need what happened in Dragon Forest to happen again. The gasses are highly flammable."

Carmen sighs as he looks down at the orange sparks between their hands. Illiana looks at their hands with wonder as she tilts her head, smiling at them. Julia catches her gaze and pulls her hand from Carmens. She doesn't want to be mean to Carmen but everyone needs to focus.

"I guess we'll scale the edges; we have to stay out of the water and stay quiet. Cypress, that means you. No drinking the water and no squeaking."

Cypress bows his head, letting out a little whimper. She walks over to him, petting his head to reassure him she isn't mad at him. He lets out a little pur as he rubs his head against her chest. Quickly, he ducks his head under her legs, flinging her onto his back. She slides back, catching the ropes around his neck that tether the wagon to him. She hugs him tight as he prances around. Everyone laughs as Julia clings on for dear life. Cypress happily hops down the trail without letting her down, and everyone follows him.

The closer they get to the swamp, the thicker the air gets. Everyone is sweating and panting as the humidity rises. The only one who seems unfazed is Cypress. These are ideal conditions for a dragon. As they approach the opening of the swamp, everyone gets quiet, only speaking in whispers and hand motions. The water is black with green swirls of algae. A light foggy mist over the swamp covers all the plants in dew. All the trees are half dead, half alive, from being waterlogged and choked out by moss. Carmen notices these rather large plants that look like large basins with lids. They are a bright yellow riddled with little red spots. The plants hang from the trees with great thick vines. The vines keep the plants just barely above the water's surface. They twist and weave through the trees with their ends draped over branches. Everyone tenses as a bird flutters over. There are soft sounds like rubbing leather and a loud snap as a vine snatches the bird out of the air, tossing it into one of the plant's open mouths. The lid shuts, trapping it. The bird screeches as it tries to escape. The plant slowly lowers to touch the water. Its yellow color thins out, becoming translucent as it fills with water. The bird screeching stops, and the plant rises, draining out all the water. Carmen covers his mouth as he slowly backs into Cypress.

"Well, this is it," Illiana whispers. She has a look of sadness on her face, unlike everyone else who looks truly terrified of what they just witnessed. Julia slides off Cypress' back and slowly tiptoes over to her.

"What's wrong? Is everything okay?" Julia speaks softly, practically mouthing the words. She takes Illiana's hands in hers. Illiana looks down at the ground. Julia places a hand on her chin to turn her head up and look into her eyes, a small tear escapes from the corner of Illiana's eye.

"Yes, my dear. You two will be perfectly fine. Please Be strong."

Julia closes her eyes, bowing her head slightly, Knowing what she means. Illiana kisses her forehead as she turns to walk down the path. Julia just stands frozen as a chill travels down her spine. Julia can feel her presence and her smugness. Her strength seems to have grown overnight. She's getting closer to them. Illiana rubs her arm with understanding. Carmen walks over, grabs her hand, and gives it a little tug to follow. She looks up at him with a half smile. He can see the tears welling in her eyes. They all walk cautiously along the swamp. Cypress sticks to the outside of everyone to keep as far away as possible. As they walk, Julia keeps hearing a whisper coming from behind them. Every time she looks back, it stops. After a while, Julia stops walking. Getting frustrated that neither Carmen nor Illiana hear the whispers as well. They all check the edge of the tree line. Nobody sees anything strange. The thick trees and bushes create a wall between the woods and the swamp. Carmen suggests it is squirrels chattering in the woods. Both Julia and Illiana shoot him an annoyed glare. Julia hears the sounds again and points in the direction they are coming from. Illiana walks over to the tree and gently waves her hands back and forth. The trees sway and creak as Illiana parts them, making it easier to see into the woods. As the opening grows, Carmen and Illiana gasp as Magnis floats between the trees. She looks completely different; her pale skin is practically wrinkle-free, her eyes are a more vibrant red, and her wiry white hair now has long, smooth curls. Carmen and Illiana look at Julia confused. They both watched her turn to dust.

"Shocked to see me?" Magnis' voice booms.

Everyone ducks, looking around as vines start reaching out to grab them. Magnis laughs. *"Don't worry, I cursed them; the only thing going to hurt you is me."* She laughs maniacally, looking around at everyone's confused expressions. *"Julia didn't tell you? I vanished before she could banish me. She hoped that by banishing the twins, I wouldn't be strong enough to fight back. It would have been smart, but she didn't take my powers. I was able to absorb the boy's powers from their stone prisons, making me stronger. Who knew being free would make me beautiful again."*

Magnis waves her hand by her face, showing off her new look. Julia takes a deep breath to let out a sonic scream. Magnis flicks her wrist, shooting her backward into the water. Magnis laughs maniacally as she flings Illiana and Carmen into some trees. Cypress shoots a long stream of fire at her, but she pushes it back towards him, burning his face. He stumbles to his feet, taking a deep breath. Quickly, she snaps her fingers, and a force field forms around him. Fire fills the space around him as he exhales. He screeches and flails in the dome. Julia is dragged out of the water into the air by a vine. She gasps for air, but the vines tighten around her neck, cutting off her oxygen.

"You guys thought you could beat me… You should think again." Magnis flicks her wrist back and forth, slamming Carmen and Illiana against some more trees, knocking them unconscious. She then rises in the air to

meet Julia's eyes. *"You didn't think I would let you die down there, did you? That would ruin all my fun."* Magnis says with laughter in her voice. She waves her hand, and the vines loosen on Julia's neck; she gasps as air returns to her lungs.

"I hope you go to hell, you fucking bitch." Julia spits in Magnis' face and struggles to escape the vines' grip. Magnis wipes her face, still smiling at her victory. *"Why didn't you bring back your idiotic twins."*

Magnis stops laughing, clenching her fist. Julia can feel her sadness for them. The vines grow tighter again, causing Julia to gasp. Magnis' face grows red with anger.

"I didn't have my spell book to free them. I tried using my connection with the book, but you knew I was still alive, so you were severing my connection to it." Magnis wipes a tear from her face. Julia can feel her love for the boys. She feels bad for her to some degree, but she knows there's no end to the fight.

*"I know you're not the monster
everyone makes you out to be. I know you are
truly kind and loving with a heart of gold."*
Julia chokes on her words as she fights for air.
*"Please, I will give you everything you want if
you let us be. No games this time."* Magnis
studies Julia's face for a moment.

She closes her eyes before muttering the
words. *"Too late."*

She waves her hand, making the vines
tighten on Julia's neck. Julia can feel the last
breath escaping from her lungs as she closes
her eyes. She feels hopeless. Her only wish is
that Illiana, Carmen, and Cypress will survive.
Her eyes tighten, welling up with tears and
blood. The world around her fades as she sees
flashbacks of her parents holding her hands
while swinging her back and forth, her parents
leaving the night they never came home, and
the scene of the accident where her parents
had been killed. Then, she sees Carmen
standing before her. He smiles big, looking so
handsome. His black hair glistens in the
sunlight, his arms flexing as he sprints to play
with Cypress. Then she sees Illiana standing

there and reaching out to her. She reaches for Illiana's hand, but everything begins to fade. The memories fade into a red blob of nothing. Julia knows this is the end. Off in the distance of the darkness, she can see a bright light growing towards her.

Nothing can save her now.

Not Carmen

Not Illiana.

No one.

It's over.

She's lost.

This is it.

Golden Hearts

Magnis stares angrily at Julia's lifeless body. She's finally won and is going to take what's rightfully hers. She stretches her hand out, placing it on Julia's arm. She squeezes her wrist. Her fingernails press into the skin, puncturing it. Magnis begins chanting

"The power of four, and nothing more. The power of four is mine to adore."

Julia's body glows green, and her power begins swirling up Magnis' arm. Magnis closes her eyes and tilts her head back. A smile creeps on her face as she sucks all the power from Julia's lifeless corpse. She flings her hand, sending Julia crashing to the ground. Carmen rolls his head slightly to pull himself into consciousness. He cries out as he runs over to Julia's body. Magnis whips around, laughing at his misery. Illiana groans on the ground as she tries lifting her body off the ground. She pulls her hair back from her face to see Carmen holding Julia in his arms. She cries out, reaching out to grab them.

"Now you see, Illiana, I can stay young forever. I can rightfully claim what is mine!" Magnis laughs as she shoots a lightning bolt next to Carmen. He looks down and up again at the close shot. He notices Cypress and shoots an energy ball at the force field. It shatters. Cypress darts out after Magnis. He smashes into her full force, sending her falling from the sky and crashing into the water. She loses all control over the vines; they shoot out from all over, grabbing at her as she flails, trying to fight back while underwater. Illiana musters all of her strength to rush over to Julia. Carmen lays his face across her chest, sobbing uncontrollably. Illiana pulls him back, holding his face between her hands. Cypress flies to their side, shooting fireballs at vines to protect them.

"There's a way to bring her back; it will take all my power. Once I do this, you and her need to run. I will take care of my sister." She looks into Carmen's eyes as a tear falls from her cheek. *"Do you understand me? You guys*

have to run, don't look back, don't try to save me."

Carmen shakes his head, trying to gather himself between sobs. Illiana runs to the turned-over wagon and rummages through the pile. She locates Julia's bag and pulls out the book of the Four Witches Clan. She thumbs through it until she finds the page she's looking for. Carmen looks at her, confused. So many questions are running through his head. *How does she know what to look for in the book? Does it matter how she knows if it brings Julia back?* Illiana places one hand over Julia's stomach and the other over her head. She closes her eyes, muttering words softly under her breath. Julia's body lifts off the ground. Carmen watches in amazement. Yellow swirls of power zip around Julia's body. Carmen shields his eyes as the power grows brighter and more intense. Julia's eyes fly open within seconds, and she drops hard to the ground. She gasps violently for air, holding her throat.

Carmen wastes no time picking Julia up to carry her to the wagon. He tips it off its side and gently places her in it. Cypress backs over, still fighting off attacking vines. Weak and dazed, Julia cries out to Illiana, who is weak on the ground, waving her hand at them to run. Carmen fills the wagon sloppily with the rest of their belongings, including Julia's spell book. He grabs the sword handle, pulling it from his side; with a hard swing, the blade extends out. Orange sparks encase it as it did before. Carmen runs to Cypress' side to help him escape the vines. He motions Cypress to the cart. Instantly, he bolts over, looping the rope around his neck. Without hesitation, they run down the path, fighting off vines.

Julia screams for Illiana as she glances back. Magnis shoots out of the water, huffing angrily while trying to catch her breath. She yells into the sky, eyes glowing red, as balls of power form at her fingertips. Magnis shoots a ball of power, hitting Illiana in the head. Her stretched-out hand drops to the ground. Julia lets out a giant sonic scream, sending Magnis soaring back into the water. The vines twitch and roar as they pull her under once again.

Julia notices her bag jumping around next to her. She pulls the flap back, and the egg jumps out, landing in Julia's hand. The egg stops jumping and starts glowing green with yellow swirls of energy. The power surrounds Julia, taking over her body. She rises up out of the cart and into the air. Carmen and Cypress skid to a halt while vines assault them. They watch with concern but are strangely comforted by the presence. Her face changes into that of someone else; it is still Julia, but it is a mature version. Julia's eyes light up green. The egg is still sitting in her hand. Julia's free hand comes up, and Magnis lifts up out of the water. She struggles to move; it looks as if a strange force is holding her captive.

"Magnis! You must pay for all the bad you have caused to my daughter and her friends." An unfamiliar voice yells from Julia's mouth. Magnis stops struggling and looks at Julia, shocked.

"Belle, it's been many years. I'm so sorry I had to kill you like that, but you betrayed us all." Magnis pleads, fear washing over her. The vines settle as Carmen and Cypress stand in shock.

"I betrayed you? You were hurting innocent people for power. You were selfish. You had good intentions, but you forgot that we are supposed to help all people. Now your time is up." Julia's hands shoot up, sending the vines rushing out of the water. They zip and swirl around Magnis, encasing her. Carmen and Cypress take this time to run over to Illiana. Once Magnis is completely encased by a ball of vines, they all simultaneously tighten, and blood trickles from the bottom of the vine mass. The egg falls to the ground, shattering. Julia snaps back into reality, drifting back to the ground. Holding her head from dizziness, she remembers Illiana and runs over. She reaches for Illiana's hand, tears streaming down her face.

"My dears, don't be sad; it is my destiny. Just remember everything I taught you." Illiana says, her voice growing weak. Julia goes to speak, but Illiana hushes her. "Listen to my words, my dear; don't forget them," Illiana says as Julia leans closer to hear her faint words. "True love is only a foot away; don't lose it." The

last words slip out of her cold, bluing lips.
With a single last breath, she fades quickly.
Her eyes stare off into the distance, empty.
Illiana's cold, lifeless hand falls from Julia's
and hits the ground gently. Carmen leans
down, grabbing Julia's shoulders to pull her
closer to him. She pulls away, touching
Illiana's heart, breathing heavily. A white light
glows under her hand, fading quickly. She yells
into the sky, repeatedly trying to bring Illiana
back. Carmen wraps his arms around her,
pulling her away. She flails her arms, punching
his leg and side. He kisses her head as she
slumps down, ending her struggle. They sit
silently for a few moments. Even Cypress, still
panting, sheds tears as he bows his head next
to Julia. She wraps her arms around his long
neck and sobs. Carmen stands up and plants
his feet firmly on the ground. He sticks his
hands out with his palms down. Slowly curling
the ends of his fingers, he turns his hands and
thrusts his palms into the air. In front of them,
a large chunk of earth lifts from the ground,
creating a deep hole. Cypress looks up, pulling
from Julia's grip. He carefully lifts Illiana's
body in his paws and gently places her into
the ground. Carmen lowers the chunk of earth

back to the ground, filling the hole. Julia sobs louder as Carmen lifts her up to place her in the wagon. Laying Julia in the wagon, Carmen looks back at the vines, still crushing Magnis. He turns, forming a large energy ball. He pushes his hands forward to destroy any remnants left of Magnis. Instead, the ball beams out, connecting him and the clump of vines. An orange glow takes over Carmen's being. Julia sits wide-eyed as she wipes away tears. Carmen's head rolls back as he pulls the green energy from the vine cluster. It forms a larger energy ball that flows back to Carmen's hands; he turns to Julia. Curiously, She reaches out to touch it. The ball of energy turns blue, trickling down Julia's arm, absorbing into her body. She takes in a deep breath as her whole being revives. All her cuts and bruises heal. Her skin and hair radiate a fresh glow. The tired circles that had formed under her eyes pop with color and life. Carmen's glow fades as he shakes his head, trying to gather what happened. He looks his hands over. He still doesn't understand this strange power or how he just transferred powers to Julia.. Julia exhales as she lays down in the wagon and continues crying.

Hours pass as they walk. Julia stays curled up in the wagon as Carmen walks alongside it, watching her. His legs slowly tire as the dark of night sets in. Cypress continues marching on, unfazed by tiredness. Carmen is amazed at Cypress' new energy; he still sees him as the cute, sleepy baby dragon that needs a nap every hour. Carmen runs forward, taping Cypress on the side, motioning that they need to find a spot to sleep. Cypress bobs his head up and down as he stops walking and collapses to the ground. He lets out a groaning sigh of air. Carmen chuckles as he pets Cypress' head. Julia pops her head up, looking around. Carmen lights a few torches, sticking them in the ground to illuminate the area. Julia points out the new moon and informs Carmen this will be the darkest night they see. Julia begins walking around, knocking on some trees. Carmen gives her a puzzled look as she inspects each tree surrounding them.

"I know you've been through hell and back today, but may I ask what you are doing?" Carmen says, sitting on a rock, watching quizzically. He doesn't understand what she's doing. Maybe she lost her mind during today's events, Carmen jokes to himself, not wanting Julia to take offense. He accidentally chuckles out loud, causing Julia to hear him. She shoots him a glare of annoyance.

"I-I-Illiana tried showing me how to bend trees. Maybe I can try to form a hut for us. It looks like it will rain; we'll need the cover." Julia winces as Illiana's name rolls past her lips. She's still fighting conflicting emotions. She went through waves of trust and distrust with Illiana, yet she gave her life to Julia. Now, with Illianas's memories flooding her head, she struggles to deal with all the emotions. All her pain, struggles, and abuse that she kept secret with her loving smile and kind-hearted nature. Carmen waves his hand at Julia as she loses herself in her thoughts again.

"Give it a try; I'm sure you can do it," Carmen says, backing up to give her space. He gives her a smile of reassurance, unaware of her internal battle. Julia gives him a half smile, hiding her pain as she sways her hands back and forth. She breathes slowly through her nose, putting all her focus on the trees. For a few moments, nothing happens, but Julia keeps trying. She closes her eyes, listening to the trees creaking, feeling the roots' vibration with her toes. After some intense concentration, the trees follow the swaying of her hands. The trees begin bending, twisting, and intertwining with each other, blending into a large dome of wood. There's an opening big enough to crawl through for a doorway. A piece of bark slides down over the opening. Vines wrap around one side, tethering it to a branch that arches over, forming the door frame. Carmen's eyes widen as he watches the hut come together.

Cypress prances around it excitedly. Julia claps her hands together and turns to look at Carmen. She smiles as a tear falls from her cheek. Illiana would have been proud of her. She marches over to the wagon, pulling out her book of spells. Carmen watches patiently as she flips through the pages. She lands on a page, slamming her finger down on it. She smiles while she marches over to her little hut. Quietly, she whispers some words, and the hut glows blue. Julia blows a kiss at the hut, and a shockwave of wind shoots out. Leaves scatter as Carmen and Cypress cover their faces. The blue glow fades, and Julia approaches the hut and pulls back the door.

"Carmen, come in; you need to see this," Julia yells from inside, her voice filled with excitement. Carmen looks up as Cypress bolts into the hut before him; he struggles to squeeze his body through the doorway that's barely big enough for him. Carmen laughs, watching him struggle as he follows in after him. Inside, Carmen's mouth drops in amazement. The inside is a huge, wide-open space. The ceiling is high enough that Cypress can fly up and sit in the rafters. To the left are two large wooden beds with vines and leaves wrapping the bottom for a springy platform to sleep on. To the back wall is a wooden table with three chairs shaped by small trees that sprout from the ground. Two chairs are smaller, perfect for Carmen and Julia, and the other is larger to fit Cypress. On the right are two shelves for books and clothing. Julia took trees and molded a perfect home in minutes. Carmen can't believe his eyes. Powers like this were unheard of in his universe.

"Julia, this is truly incredible! Illiana would be so proud of you. I know I am." Carmen runs over to the bed and falls back onto it. Julia walks to the other side of the bed and falls back beside him. They lay there staring at the ceiling. Carmen reaches his hand up to touch hers. Carmen can feel the orange sparks as their hands touch. His mind floods with information, he instantly rolls to face her. His eyes widen with hurt and realization he has been deceived.

"Illiana was part of the four witches! That's how she knew what to look for in your book. That's why she was looking for us. She was after the same thing her sister was." Carmen tries not to sound panicked or upset but is shocked that Julia has kept this information from him. He knew he felt uneasy about her but wasn't sure what had caused it. Julia closes her eyes, and a tear squeezes out and rolls down her face to her ear. Carmen wipes the tear away, pushing her hair behind her ear.

"It's more complicated than that. She wanted power, but it had nothing to do with me. She wanted to mend things with Magnis.

She had only joined when she found her hoping things would get better. She was forced out when Magnis rejected her. She came to us to stop her when she discovered she was hell-bent on returning honor to their family, but that couldn't happen. If she had freed the dragons, there would be mass chaos and destruction, and no one could stop it."

Carmen rolls back, looking up at the ceiling, his mind boggled. Julia sighs as she reaches for Carmen's hand again.

"Many of her memories and knowledge were transferred to me when she saved me. It's almost like part of her is in me. I keep reliving her pain and suffering. I can't seem to find too many happy moments. I know you struggled to trust her, and she lied to us. She had good intentions, but sadly, so did her sister. She just didn't understand the aftermath that would ensue." Julia rolls to face him again, resting her head on his chest. Carmen gently strokes her hair as they lay there in silence.

"I can't pretend to know what you are going through right now. But I promise, you don't need to do this alone."

Julia lets herself smile as she buries her face in his shirt, wiping tears from her eyes. Slowly, they drift to sleep, entangled with one another. Cypress drops down from the rafters and slowly crawls into bed. He lays around Carmen and Julia, touching his nose to his tail. Now, big enough, his form creates a perfect ring around them.

Am I Dreaming?

"**G**ood Afternoon, sleepy; come sit and have lunch," Carmen says calmly.

He looks at Julia with a wide smile as he gestures to the sandwiches on the table. Julia rubs her head as she gets out of bed and wanders to the table. She picks up one of the sandwiches and takes a bite. She feels oddly tired given that it's lunchtime. *Did she really sleep all that time?* After a few minutes, Carmen waves his hand to the door. Julia turns her head, and the room fades around her.

They are now outside; Carmen stands by two trees perfectly apart with a hammock tethered to them. Cautiously, Julia walks over and gets in. She places her head on the pillow and looks up at Carmen as he gently rocks her side to side. She closes her eyes, feeling oddly relaxed. She feels a cool breeze rush over her. Taking a deep breath through her nose, she can smell the sweet mist of the ocean. It's so peaceful and calm. Something's off, but she's too hazy to figure it out. She hears another voice on the other side of her, but it isn't Carmen's.

She opens her eyes and screams in fear. She is no longer in the hammock; she is now standing in a cage surrounded by dragons flying around her. She looks up to see Cypress flying above her, holding the cage in his large claws. She reaches forward to grab the bars as a sudden pain shoots down her back. She reaches back, feeling the handle of a dagger. She winces in pain, crying as she slowly pulls it from her back. She opens her mouth to yell for Carmen, but nothing comes out. She slaps her hands over her mouth.

The door to the cage flings open sending her tumbling into the open air. She closes her eyes tight as she lands with a bounce on the hard, cold ground. She slowly opens her eyes and is in the hut again on the bed. She looks around and feels the small of her back where the dagger once was.

She sees Illiana walk into the hut. Her hands tied behind her back. She is shoved and falls to the ground. Magnis walks in behind her with a large smile. Julia lets out a scream as

Magnis flings Carmen's sword at her head. "STOP!" The words echo in the hut as Magnis freezes in place. Illiana rolls to her knees, waiting for Julia. Julia scrambles out of the bed to Illiana.

"My dear, help me, please. I need your help, dear. I am stuck."

Julia places a hand on Illiana's cheek.

"How are you stuck? You're right in front of me."

Illiana raises her hands, placing one on Julia's forehead and the other on her chest. She taps her head repeatedly. "I don't understand." Julia places her hand on Illiana's.

"In here, my dear. You need to find me."

Julia shakes her head, confused. Illiana lets out a pained scream as she shoves Julia back against the bed.

She jolts awake, breathing heavily, covered in sweat. Carmen rushes over with a bowl in hand. He sits in front of her, wrapping his arms around her. She curls into his chest, breaking out in sobs. Cypress rushes over, sticking his head between them and resting it on her lap. He lets out a soft squeak as she hugs his face.

"We got you. It's alright. It was just a bad dream." Carmen strokes her head gently with one hand as he awkwardly holds the bowl of eggs in the other. Julia pulls back a little, not wanting to open her eyes. Carmen wipes the tears off her face, pulling her hair back tucking it behind her ear.

"Are you sure I'm awake? It felt so real." Julia opens one eye slightly to inspect. She can see the bowl of eggs in Carmen's hands. She grabs it quickly and shovels the food into her mouth. She has never felt so hungry before. Carmen shoots her a small smile of reassurance as he chuckles. She closes her eyes as she lowers her spoon into the bowl. Carmen lets out another small chuckle as he heads back to the table to grab the map. Julia looks around, still dazed; everything has been packed except the map and Julia's spell book. Carmen spent the morning straightening out all their supplies after being tossed around the day before. Julia reaches out for the map as she slurps down a spoonful of eggs. Carmen pulls the map back as he shakes his head. He playfully waves a finger at her before pointing at her eggs. Julia smiles, shaking her head at him. She continues eating eggs, feeling more at peace knowing she is awake.

"Now that you're a map expert, where to next?" Julia asks, giggling at her own joke. Carmen smiles big as he pokes at the map.

"It looks like we're going to Dragon Castle." Carmen says excitedly. Cypress jumps around, squealing and squeaking with joy. Julia laughs as she pulls her bowl to her chest to keep it from spilling. Carmen and Cypress jump around together. Cypress lifts Carmen off the ground as he holds his hand. Julia giggles at their childlike merriment.

"Just a few more miles, and we can go home!"

Carmen stops jumping around snapping a big smile at Julia. Quickly, he shoves the map into the bag on the table and runs over to the bed. He hops over to Julia on his hands and knees, looking into her eyes. She giggles at his excitement.

"Does that mean you and Cypress are coming with me?" Carmen's eyes widen as he waits for her response. His smile can't get any bigger, as his cheeks turn red.

Julia smiles as she bows her head, letting her hair fall in her face. "Carmen, what do you think Illiana meant when she said true love is only a foot away? Don't lose it?"

Carmen sits back slightly as his face softens, still holding his smile.

"I've been thinking about what she said, and I know what it means to me, and I think it means the same thing to you. I can see most of her memories, so I know what she thought when she said it." Julia speaks softly as she looks down at her hands. It's quiet for a moment as Julia feels her heart beating out of her chest. Slowly, she looks up and peeks through her hair at Carmen. His face is soft as his eyes smile back at her. Slowly, he reaches up, pushing her hair out of her face and behind her ears. He gently touches her chin as he pulls her face closer to his. He clears his throat as he whispers to her.

"We've only known each other for a short while, but our souls have known each other for an eternity." Carmen leans in slowly. Julia can feel her heart jumping out of her chest as their lips press together. Cypress lets out a loud screech as he bolts across the room and out the door. Julia and Carmen pull back and look at each other as they laugh out of embarrassment. They completely forgot that he was in the room. Julia hangs her head, letting her hair fall as warmth brushes over her face. Carmen kisses the top of her head as he pushes himself out of the bed.

"We should get going; we're so close," Julia says, blushing. She wants nothing more than to stay here with Carmen but she is ready to make a home with him in his universe. She loves the fact that Cypress will be going with them. They grab the bags off the table and head out the door. Cypress stands at the wagon, ready to go. He gives them a look as he shakes his head. They laugh, throwing the bags into the wagon. Julia pulls out her spell book and starts flipping through the pages. She holds a hand out to the hut and begins whispering. Like the night before, the hut glows

blue, shaking and creaking. The vines unweave from the bark door, and the bark molds to its original form. They all watch the trees unwrap and untangle from each other. Carmen stares in amazement as their little hut vanishes like it was never there.

"You really have a handle on your powers now?" Carmen says, grabbing Julia's hand. She smiles big as she sets off down the path with him. She hugs his arm, smiling to herself. She feels happy knowing she gets to explore a new life with Carmen and go on new adventures with him and Cypress. She finally has a family again, and it's perfect.

She gets a newfound knowledge on how to control her powers and a spell book to help her out, thanks to Illiana. Deep down, she can't help but feel sadness for Illiana and Magnis. She sees both sides of their stories and wishes there was a way to make them understand each other. Maybe things could have been different between them. Maybe they could still be alive; maybe they could have come to live in Carmen's universe and get a new start. Maybe they could have found a solution for their people to live somewhere they didn't need to hide in fear for their lives. Having Illiana's memories makes her want to make everything better and fix the wrongs that have been done. But there's no chance of that now. She can feel the guilt of the sisters, but she hides it deep inside so Carmen doesn't doubt how happy she is to move forward with her life. She hopes there is a spell in the book to separate Illianas emotions from her own.

Dragon Castle

They walk several miles before approaching a large stone wall with a gate. The wall is made of large white and light gray stones with black stones placed in a swirling pattern periodically. The gate has steel plates with large rivets lining it up and down, holding the wooden planks in place. The gate is about twenty feet tall. In the middle of the giant gate is a huge keyhole. Cypress crouches down low as he notices two large green dragons perched high on the side of the wall, standing guard. He recognizes them from their attack in Dragon Forest. One of them has a large scar from where Carmen had stabbed him. He squeezes between Carmen and Julia, shaking. They stroke his head, reassuring him they can't harm him outside the forest. The two dragons watch closely as they walk slowly to the gate.

"Holt, who goes there?" says a deep scratchy voice. Carmen and Julia look at each other.

"It's Carmen, Julia, and Cypress. We are here to speak with the dragon ki-."

"I know why you're here; it took you long enough. When you enter, wait for Prince Hugh to escort you." The voice interrupts. There is a loud bang as tumblers start turning. The door starts slowly opening with a loud squeal. They cover their ears as the three of them stand there confused. They walk in cautiously. At first, they don't see anyone or anything; they just see another rock wall. A short man with brown hair drops down from the side of the wall in front of them. His eyes sparkle a deep brown. He's frowning behind his thick red beard, but he doesn't seem sad; he's just annoyed. Julia curtsies as Carmen and Cypress bow their heads.

"The king has been expecting you for some time now; he will be glad to hear that you have finally arrived," the man says with an agitated voice, walking them to another big door. He sighs between each word, emphasizing his annoyance. Julia scowls at his disrespect. He hasn't greeted them at all. *How rude? Is this Prince Hugh? He didn't bow back, and he rolled his eyes at them.*

"Excuse me, sir. Are you Hugh? How did the King know we were coming?" Julia asks, running ahead to stop him from continuing down the corridor. The man takes a deep breath, rolling his eyes.

"Four weeks ago, the King's visionary, Illiana, told us three would be coming for the Dragon King's help, Blah Blah Blah. Now, if you're done being rude, it's not my job to answer your annoying questions." He waves his hands, shoeing Julia away. Carmen and Julia look at each other with wide eyes. Hearing her name freezes them in their tracks. She hadn't mentioned working for the King. Julia hasn't seen any information within her memories about it.

"How did she manage to hide this from us?" Julia whispers. Carmen shakes his head and shrugs as they continue forward. He grabs Julia's hand to comfort her with Cypress trailing behind. The man brings them through a series of halls and large galleries before coming to a large white and gold door. On the left half is a carving of a dragon bowing to the right. On the right half, there's a carving of what looks to be a king and queen bowing to the left. The grumpy man whistles a small tune while tapping on the door. They hear footsteps approaching on the other side as the door swings open. The three stand there in awe at the beautiful sight. The man rolls his eyes and clears his throat.

"Are you coming in, or are you going to waste our time? I'd rather not stand here all day." He waves them through the door. They enter a large white room with various plants and green and blue tapestries hanging along the walls. The floor is white and black marble, with a red and gold carpet that runs to a set of steps leading up to a platform. On the platform are eight large thrones. The thrones are sorted by titles. The Human King and Dragon King are in the middle, with their queens to their respective sides and the Princes/Princesses on the outer edges.

In the Dragon King's spot is a gorgeously terrifying purple and red dragon with long horns. He watches over his long snout with his head held high. Julia looks at him in awe. He's the most enormous, majestic dragon she's ever seen; his colors are so vibrant. As they reach the platform, they bow. The Dragon King remains seated as his gaze locks onto Cypress. The Human King and Queen rise from their thrones. The Queen walks over to the man and kisses him on the forehead. Julia let out a slight snort, shaking her head. *He is Prince Hugh.*

"Thank you, my son, for delivering our guest to us."

Hugh rolls his eyes and wanders to his throne on the far right. Smiling, she shakes her head at him, trying to hide her annoyance.

"Welcome to our kingdom. Our visionary told us you'd be coming. It's been a long time since we had a visitor from outside our universe." She turns to look at Carmen, who gulps nervously.

Still studying the Dragon King in awe, Julia tightens her grip on Carmen's hand.

"I am Queen Myah Jollyman, and This is King Martin Jollyman. Although we are the King and Queen for the Human side of our alliance with the dragons, we are only here to meet you and wish you well on your journey."

Carmen's eyes widen. *"So you're not going to help me get home?"* Carmen's voice breaks with sadness.

The Queen shakes her head with a chuckle. *"Oh No, my dear, we can not help you. However, the Dragon King may help you if he wishes."* The Queen turns, motioning to the Dragon King. *"This is King Rupert Kilmaliki. He is the wisest, most powerful dragon. He is who you must convince to help you."* The Human King and Queen leave with a bow and curtsy. Prince Hugh remains on his throne as he glares, annoyed at their presence. The Dragon King slowly lowers his head, keeping his sight on Cypress.

"Sir, if I may, I- I - I-" Carmen stutters as King Rupertinterrupts.

"I know why you are here and what you want. Our visionary told us everything; I see she got you here safely. The last time someone visited our universe from another, my father was killed defending us. Men from a disappearing door kept coming here and taking all our supplies and killing our women and children. I will not make the same mistake. I will help you get home to protect our kingdom." King Rupert speaks with a deep,

slow voice. It's stern but oddly calming. Carmen is confused by what the King is saying. He's assuming the events the King talks about have to do with Domonic's doors. There's never been any information about life within the universe.

Are there secrets being kept by the three kingdoms? Is Domonic the evil man all the literature describes him as? The events happened over 200 years ago. How could it have been the Dragon King's father that died?

Carmen doesn't know much about dragons, but surely 200 years would be a long time to live. Unless time between Universes works differently. Rather than days. *Has Carmen been gone for weeks or months?* So many questions swirl in his mind, but he just bows with a half smile. He doesn't want to ask questions that may upset King Rupert. He begins thanking him profusely.

"I wasn't done speaking." His voice booms as he breaks his gaze on Cypress for the first time. He slowly gets up from his throne and thuds down the steps to greet Julia face-to-face. Carmen pulls her arm closer to him for support. *"How did you manage to*

obtain a baby dragon? How dare you treat him like he is a pet. Are your plans to kill him when he's bigger?"

Cypress lets out a little shriek as he looks to Julia for an answer. Julia trembles for a moment as the King Rupert snorts smoke in her face.

"I would never!" Julia musters up as a scream, appalled by his accusations. "He is not a pet. He is family, and he is all I have. Hunters killed his mother on the southeast side of the island. He was just an egg, and I took him in before they could kill him, too." Julia reaches over, hugging Cypress around the neck. The dragon king pulls back.

For a moment, there's shock on his face. It fades quickly as he sternly leans back in. "Very well then. Tomorrow afternoon, I will face you with a few challenges. If you are successful, I will let you go home. If you are not, you'll die, and my problem will be solved."

Prince Hugh laughs with entertainment. King Rupert turns his head to him, letting out a low growl. He quickly throws his head in his hands to hide his laughter..

"Thank you, sir. We appreciate all your help, and the three of us can get through anything together." Carmen bows his head as he smiles at Julia and Cypress.

"NO!" King Rupert's voice booms with a harshness. "You will not have the aid of your dragon companion. He will sit with me. I will not risk a fellow dragon for the likes of a human that does not belong here! As for the two of you, you can help each other with some tasks, but not all. There will be parts you must do on your own. Failure to comply will result in your death! Hugh, take them to their rooms and prepare them for dinner."

Prince Hugh sighs as he rolls from his throne and lazily thuds down the steps to escort them to their rooms. Quietly, they turn to follow him.

"One last thing before you go. I would like your dragon friend Cypress to report to my quarters before dinner. I want to chat with him to ensure he has been cared for properly." He looks back over at Cypress, who is studying him again.

Julia clenches her fist as she turns to King Rupert. "I would never harm him! I love him!"

King Rupert lets out a loud rumbling roar as his head raises. He shoots out a purple flame across the ceiling. He then arches down, slamming his front paws on the ground. The room shakes, and Julia stumbles back into Carmen's arms. *"I SAID WHAT I SAID; NOW LEAVE BEFORE I CHANGE MY MIND AND EAT YOU!"*

The three turn and head for the door, where Hugh continues walking as if nothing is happening.

Once the door shuts, Julia looks at Carmen and asks, *"What does he want with Cypress?"* Carmen shrugs. They both look at Cypress, who's walking with his head low behind Hugh, trying to hide.

As they venture through the twists and turns of the dully-lit maze-like halls, they admire the large paintings of past Kings, Queens, and others in the royal families. Prince Hugh stops in the middle of the hall and points to the three doors to his left.

"These are your rooms. They join in the middle if you would like. However, it is frowned upon for men and women to share rooms when

unwed. The punishment is harsh..... Please feel free to share a room so I can enjoy some entertainment." Hugh cracks a small smile and chuckles as he continues down the hall away from them. Julia rolls her eyes as she enters the first room with Cypress and Carmen close behind.

"For a Prince, he doesn't seem very friendly," Julia says, listening to his footsteps through the door. Carmen shakes his head in agreement as he hops into the giant bed in the center of the room. The curtains that hang around the bed wave as the bed bounces. Cypress runs, jumping into the bed after him. Carmen rolls quickly to not get crushed. Julia laughs, shaking her head at them, and runs to jump in. They all laugh as they roll together in the center of the bed. Julia stops quickly, sitting up with a serious look.

"I wonder why the King wants to speak with Cypress. It's not like he's been mistreated. He's clean, healthy, and strong."

Carmen shrugs as he props up on his elbows. Cypress sticks his head up high, puffing out his chest as Julia lists all the great things about him. They chuckle together.

"He was so focused on him, it was kinda terrifying. I get his best interest is in the well-being of dragons, but the point of the two kings is to bring a union between humans and dragons. You would think he'd be happy that I a human, I took him in and actually took care of him instead of leaving him to die." Julia sighs, tapping her finger on her leg. Cypress scooches over to Julia, nestling his head on her lap. She sighs happily as she smiles and leans down to kiss his head. They all lay snuggled in the large bed to rest.

Carmen and Julia drift to sleep in the comfort of the bed. Neither of them was tired, but it was so nice to relax and rest. Cypress lay awake, waiting for an opportunity to be brave and carefully slip away to wander the halls.

Royal Lost and Found

His curiosity about what King Rupert wants with him is getting to him. He creeps to the door, quietly shutting it behind him. As he walks Cypress sticks close to the wall not wanting to disrupt those working. Cypress awkwardly bows and smiles at them, but no one bows or smiles back. Trying to keep his spirits up, he focuses on all the paintings on the walls. In his short life, he has never seen such beautiful paintings, especially ones with dragons. The few he had seen in Dracfalls only depicted dragons being slain by humans or laying dead as humans stood on them in victory-like trophies. But these are different; dragons and humans stand side by side or share a dinner together. No fighting, no war, no violence to dragons or humans.

He stops quickly. A large door with carvings catches his interest. It has carvings of a large dragon in armor. He's standing on a hill with fire blazing all around him. Something's drawing Cypress to the door, so he gives it a great big push. Inside is King Rupert. He's sitting at an abnormally large desk with a feather pen writing in a book. He turns his head to Cypress, startled by the sound of him opening the door. King Rupert flashes him a great big smile.

"I hoped you would venture out into the castle to find me. I didn't want to have to send guards to bring you to me. My goal was not to scare you." King Rupert gets up from his desk and walks around to Cypress. Cypress bows his head, scared of what the King might want. King Rupert takes Cypress' head in his paws, tilts it side to side, and examines him.

"Does that girl treat you well? Does she feed you well? You don't look malnourished so that's a good sign." King Rupert lets go of Cypress' face as he nods frantically. "Good, I'm glad to hear some humans can have a heart towards us dragons; most don't. Can you speak, boy?" Cypress shakes his head as he looks at the ground. "Ah, I see. Curious, tho." King Rupert closes his eyes, placing a paw on Cypress' forehead. Cypress' eyes widen as he hears the King's voice. "I want to tell you a story. My wife

and I had been waiting for a fertile egg. It took
years and years, but finally, we had just one
fertile out of the clutch. The egg was so warm
with life, we were so excited. Typically, with
dragon eggs, you can hear the baby inside and
communicate with it before it hatches.
However, no sounds came from our egg
despite its warmth.

One night, while my queen slept, I cradled
the egg in my arms, hoping for any sign that
things would be ok and we would have a
healthy baby. As I touched the egg to my face,
a miracle happened. Flashes of sounds flooded
my brain. They were sounds the baby was
hearing from inside the egg. I could hear
myself talking to my young. I could hear my
sweet queen singing her lullabies. I woke my
wife to show her our baby was special.
Telepathy in dragons is rare, but they are
usually the most powerful. We were so blessed
that we could now communicate with our baby.
We spent the next few months communicating
back and forth, listening to its memories. I
never left the castle as I never wanted to miss
anything. However, issues arose.

A few weeks ago, the human King and I
went to a small village on the island's
southeast side. My wife, who was here with our
egg, got impatient as I was late coming back.
She decided to venture out to find me. She
slipped past the guards so they wouldn't stop

or follow her. She was always so stubborn yet so brave. As she neared the village, hunters struck her down, perishing before she even hit the ground. When we found her, she had been ripped apart, and our precious egg was nowhere to be seen. I blamed myself for leaving her knowing her stubbornness, but that's why I fell in love with her. She had no fear and was always full of adventure.

I feared the worst for our egg but knew I could do nothing. I had our visionary search for it. She could feel its energy in the village, but then she felt it crack and lost the connection. I feared the worst until today." King Rupert opens his eyes to see Cypress staring at him in shock. His smile falls as he sighs. Cypress slowly lifts his paw, wiping a tear from the King's cheek. He places his paw on the King's forehead and closes his eyes. With a deep breath, Cypress starts humming in his head. He remembers hearing it from within his egg but has yet to learn its origin. The King smiles as he hears the tune in his head.

Then the voice humming the tune changes, and in the darkness of Cypress' eyelids, an image of Julia flashes. She was humming the tune while rocking him in a basket. Then, another of Carmen and Julia humming it while walking as Cypress crunched pinecones. King Rupert laughs a deep, hardy chuckle. *"That's a great family you have there, my boy. They really do love and adore you."* Cypress' eyes fly open. He studies the King for a moment. He tilts his head, thinking how he knew he was thinking of Julia and Carmen. King Rupert smiles again. *"My boy, you just showed me them. That's how I knew you were thinking of them. You can connect with others and show them what you want to say. Not only can they hear your memories, but they can also see what you have seen. It's a beautiful gift you have, one of many."* Cypress ducks his head, scared. Julia told him and Carmen that dragons with multiple abilities get killed. He flashes the memory, hoping his father will see it. *"Yes, This is true, my boy. But your secret is safe with me. As much as I would love for you to stay here with me, I know it would not be safe for you. You must go with your friends. Even being the King's son, you will be seen as a threat and put to death. I will not let that happen as long as I live. You will be safe with them, and once Carmen learns his full potential, you can visit anytime."* King Rupert smiles wide. Cypress half smiles back. He's still confused but happy to know he has a father.

King Rupert takes Cypress around the castle, talking to him for a few hours. Cypress shows his memories of their adventure to the castle and all they had to overcome. They laugh at Carmen and Julia's undeniable love for each other. They even share a tear or two as King Rupert gets to watch the memories of Cypress' hatching and growth. He's honored that Julia has given him so much love. No other human would have done the same. Cypress eventually questions the tasks the King is going to put them through. King Rupert reassures him that the tasks are nothing more than to help them on their path and there is no real danger. Carmen needs an extra push to unlock his full potential to go home. The King sends Cypress to get Julia and Carmen for dinner as it's getting late.

When he gets there, Julia and Carmen aren't in the bed where he had left them. With a small whimper, he wanders to the dining hall, hoping they have already made their way to dinner.

In the dining hall, Carmen and Julia sit side by side. The table is large enough to seat 30 people and is lined with food. Cypress squeals as he dives into a platter loaded with fish and lobster. Carmen and Julia dig into a giant pig roast covered in apple slices. They have been the only ones in the dining hall for a while. Slowly, The Kings and Queens join in as well. Prince Hugh grumpily wanders in last, taking one of the empty seats at the end furthest from everyone else. Maids and servants make their way around the table, clearing empty plates and refilling glasses, each bowing to Cypress while muttering *"Your Majesty"* before clearing away old items and replacing them with something new. Cypress lowers his head, getting uncomfortable with all the newfound attention and glances. He tries to eat quickly, but Carmen and Julia give him weird, questioning looks. They watch him as they eat but don't bother asking their questions in front of the royal personnel. Everyone eats quietly until King Rupert clears his throat.

"I would like to make a toast. Tomorrow starts a new day with new adventures. Carmen and Julia, I wish you luck with your challenges. May you learn everything you need so you can survive them." He gives them a wink and turns to Cypress. *"Although my excitement got the best of me, and most of you already know. I*

would like to welcome home my beautiful baby boy. Your mother would be so proud."

Carmen spits his wine across the table covering Prince Hugh. CAusing everyone to chuckle. Prince Hugh shoots a daggering glare at Carmen as he wipes his face. Julia sits staring at Cypress, her eyes wide and mouth hung open. Cypress frantically looks at the two of them and back at the King. He bows his head, embarrassed at the attention.

Now, it makes sense to him why the staff is treating him better now than when they first saw him in the halls. Cypress turns his head back to Carmen and Julia and gives them a nervous smile and a shrug. Neither of them blinks as they stare in shock. Everyone cheers and claps, including the Human King and Queen. Cypress starts hyperventilating from embarrassment and runs out of the dining hall. Carmen and Julia chase after him, and the dining hall is left in complete silence.

In the room, Cypress lies on the bed, exhausted, trying to catch his breath. Julia sits next to him and starts rubbing his belly to sooth him. She can tell he is bothered by the

King's announcement. Cypress curls into a ball, placing his head in her lap.

"Cypress, I know you're going through a lot right now. This is big news for all of us. When I picked up your egg that night, I had no idea you were the Dragon Prince. I just knew you needed love and care."

Cypress sits up and turns to face Julia. He closes his eyes and focuses on connecting with Carmen and Julia. He visualizes his conversation with his father and focuses on pushing it to them. His eyes open as the memory plays out in his head. He smiles big as he watches Carmen's and Julia's faces light up. Although shocked and confused, they smile at him. Julia cries while listening to his father's story but then smiles as he talks about how loved and safe he is with them. Waves of emotions wash over them. Next, he pushes memories of him and them playing and laughing together. Carmen laughs as he watches himself try to teach Cypress how to juggle fire balls and accidentally catches a bush on fire. They are amazed at what they're seeing. It is like a third party watching them up close, like a movie of themselves. Julia smiles big, reaching for his head. Cypress bows his head, and Julia kisses him on the forehead.

"I love you too, buddy. I am so glad you're part of our family."

Cypress lets out a squeak as he rubs his head against hers. She leans down, hugging him tight. Cypress pulls back, letting out a big yawn, and stretches, arching his back like a cat and stretching out his claws. He twirls around to get comfy as he plops his body in the middle of the bed, curling into a ball. His tail flops over his face to block out the light. Julia shakes her head as she snuggles beside him, using his paw and arm as a pillow. Carmen takes a minute, watching them drift to sleep. He grabs a blanket to cover Julia before blowing out the candles that light the room. He lays before Cypress, using Julia's legs as his pillow. He smiles, knowing he has found happiness. He focuses on their breathing as he drifts to sleep.

Secrets

There is a loud banging on the door; Carmen and Cypress flail in the bed, startled awake by the sudden noise. Carmen runs to the door as the banging gets louder and harder. He pulls the door open fast to see Prince Hugh standing there. He has the same annoyed and unamused look on his face as yesterday.

"About time you answer the damn door. The lady of the room has already gone down for breakfast, I suggest you head down or not; I really don't care. But the King will be expecting you soon for your first task." Prince Hugh rolls his eyes as he walks off. Carmen turns back to see Cypress hiding in the beams of the ceiling. He shakes his head, laughing as he waves him down. Carmen taunts him for being a scaredy cat, and Cypress shoves him over, letting out a small laughing squeak as he runs down the hall. Carmen jumps up, chasing after him. Maids and guards jump out of their way as the two carelessly chase each other through the halls. Every time Carmen gets close, Cypress flies up into the vaulted ceilings to get away before coming back down.

In the dining hall, Cypress runs to the table, digging into the food. Carmen looks around to find Julia, but she isn't there. He eagerly digs into the mounds of food set on the table. His mouth drools as he scans over the table; bacon, ham, sausage, and potato piles line the table. Cypress has already helped himself to some eggs and pigs' feet. Carmen grimaces at the pigs' feet but shrugs it off. He is a dragon, after all; their diets typically consist of whole animals, so it only makes sense he'd like the food only some humans have an acquired taste for.

Carmen sits, placing a napkin on his lap. As he leans forward to eat, he is startled by two pale arms reaching over him and pulling him backwards. He slams back in the chair and cranes his neck to see Julia smiling over him. She leans in to kiss his cheek as he catches his breath.

"Good morning, handsome. Did I scare you?" Julia laughs as she takes the seat next to him.

Carmen lets out a big sigh as he smiles back at her.

"Good morning beautiful, you look well rested. I take it you slept well?" Julia laughs, batting her eyes at him as she nods slightly. Cypress groans, while rolling his eyes at them. He obnoxiously slurps a string of deer intestine knowing it would get under Carmen's skin. They all eat in peace for a few moments, laughing and joking around, until there's a loud bang from the door slamming open. Hugh bursts into the room and storms over to the table grumpily. He takes the chair at the end, plopping himself down hard. Leaning back, he lumps his feet on the table and snaps his fingers. A large woman hurries out of the kitchen with a plate. She hands the plate to Hugh and pulls back, scared as if she is going to be hit. She hovers for a few moments before being waved away by Hugh. Realizing everyone is staring at him, he raises his eyebrows and waves his hand at the table.

"Well, eat! It's not like you have all day or you can starve. I don't care, but hell, stop watching me like a peasant while I eat."

They all turn their heads to their plates to finish so they can leave quickly. Hugh seems to always bring an unwelcoming presence everywhere he goes. Cypress finishes quickly and bolts out the door without a second look back. Carmen keeps his head down as he eats. Julia eats little bites at a time, eyeing Hugh, annoyed with his rude mannerisms. His feet remain on the table, and his boots are covered in dirt and mud. He takes large bites and breathes obnoxiously through his mouth with each chew. Julia thinks to herself; it *sounds like he is making love with his food with those grunts and groans.* She cringes at the idea. She shakes her head a bit as she feels anger washing over her. This isn't like her to get angry at others' mannerisms no matter how repulsive. Unless impeding on her life she can usually ignore others and just keep to herself. She shoves a spoonful of eggs into her mouth before taking a deep breath. Hugh lets out more grunts and snorts as he eats. She places her hand down gripping the edges of her plate as one of Illiana's memories takes over her thoughts. She can see Hugh pushing around some maids as he waits for his food. He scolds them with the most foul language for not being prepared for his arrival to the dining hall. One maid cowers on the floor pleading with him. She apologizes profusely exclaiming he was much too early but they would work quickly to fetch him some food. Hugh raises a hand to her and Julia can hear Illiana's voice yelling at him to leave them be. He stands from his seat, hurling an empty plate in her direction. Julia ducks as the memory fades and reality resurfaces. She slams her fists on the table hard as she stands up.

"For a prince of the land, you are absolutely repulsive and disrespectful. You are meant to represent the people and the land and give hope for our future." Her fist clench tighter with anger as a smile flashes across Hughs face. There is silence as Hugh continues chewing his food. Carmen tugs at Julia's arm to pull her back into her seat. She rips her arm from his grasp, letting out a small snort of anger. Her eyes lock on Hugh as he leans further back in his chair and dabs his mouth with a cloth the maid brought him.

"Well, sweetheart, lucky for me, how I act doesn't matter. My brother is next in line for the throne, and unlike him I can't leave the castle, so I don't have to care or impress anyone, including the likes of a peasant like you or your ugly ass boyfriend."

Julia kicks her chair back as she lunges around the table after him. Carmen grabs her around the waist, dragging her towards the door. Flailing her legs and arms, she lets out a small sonic scream. Hugh, who is laughing, flies back out of the chair and tumbles to the floor. Two maids slam the door shut as Carmen and Julia exit the room. They fall to the floor as Julia continues to struggle.

Hugh from the other side of the door yells, "Get me that peasant, I want her dead!" Julia lays back on the floor, chuckling in her small victory as Carmen glares at her.

"Are you crazy? You're gonna get us kicked out or killed. This isn't like you."

Julia waves a hand at him as if to silence him. Carmen rolls his eyes as he sticks out a hand to help her. "They aren't going to do anything. If you haven't noticed, they shut us out to protect us, and they haven't opened the door to come get me. He treats the help like shit, so they're going to play dumb and dance around his commands."

Carmen raises his eyebrow, annoyed by her outburst. Julia scoffs with a smile at the door; they can still hear Hugh yelling through the door. She takes his hand pulling herself up to head down the hall back to their rooms.

Carmen plops down on the bed in the room, staring off at the ceiling. Julia sits next to him, studying his face.

"You gotta admit that was pretty funny. The look on his face when he fell back was priceless. I'm pretty sure one of the maids giggled."

Carmen shakes his head with a slight smile. "I guess he deserved it, he is an ass." Carmen looks over at Julia as they burst out into laughter together. "It doesn't matter his title or him being mistreated by his family; others shouldn't suffer due to his misery."

Julia raises her eyebrows, nodding. She brushes Carmen's hair back as she gets up and wanders to the window. She looks over the wide-open land. There are large shrubs sculpted into shapes of people and dragons. Gardens of thousands of bright flowers, colors so vivid. She sees a small pond surrounded by dragons. Smiling, she frantically waves Carmen over. At the pond, a group of young dragons split up into groups with the King. It's like they are in class. Cypress sits in one group. They all shoot fireballs at a target, and when the group finishes, all the dragons clap and cheer for each other. Although they are smaller dragons, the clapping makes a loud rumble that can be felt throughout the castle walls. The next group steps forward; they all line up and shoot water balls at the targets. Julia realizes the groups are divided by power type. Julia's eyes widen, looking at Cypress, who excitedly rushes over to join in.

"CYPRESS NO!" Julia screams out the window. All the dragons look up at them. The King scowls at her, annoyed with her outburst. Without a second thought, Julia jumps from the window to the ground. Carmen lunges forward, watching her fall to the ground. Just before hitting the ground, Julia lets out a sonic scream that pushes her up slightly, allowing

her to land safely on the ground. Carmen scrambles to the bedroom door, not wanting to follow out the window. Outside, Julia races to the group. She slows slightly, trying to catch her breath as she nears. King Rupert roars loudly as he stomps through the group towards Julia.

"How dare you interrupt our lesson. These lessons are crucial to the developing minds of young dragons."

Julia falls back on her butt as he sticks his face in hers. She can feel the warmth pouring out his nose as he snorts. Julia takes a big gulp, still trying to catch her breath. Carmen, breathing heavily from taking the long way out, rushes to Julia's side, helping her up.

"Sir, she wasn't trying to be rude; she just didn't want Cypress to over-exert his ability," Carmen says the last word with extra emphasis. He pulls Julia's hand, pulling her closer to him. The King pulls back, and his eyes soften. He looks over at Cypress, who is trying to hide poorly in the back of the group despite him being slightly larger than the others. With a sigh, King Rupert knows exactly what they are referring to and is thankful that his son's secret is being kept safe.

"Group, we will disburse for today; good job, everyone, keep practicing. We will meet here at the same time tomorrow."

All the young dragons crouch down and leap into the air, flying off. Each one says *thank you* as they depart. Now more exposed, Cypress slowly walks over to them with his head down. "My boy, they are right. We can't risk you exposing your other powers. While here on the island, you can only be present as fire. We don't want to risk anyone finding out, even other dragons."

Cypress nods with understanding. The King turns his focus back to the out-of-breath Julia.

"Thank you for protecting and loving him. You have done something unheard of in the dragon world, and it means a lot to me."

Julia smiles as she bows her head.

"It makes me feel like my work to bring peace between us is actually doing something."

"Sir, My mother taught me that kindness lives in all things, including the earth and sky. Treat it respectfully, and great things will return to you."

"Your mother was a wise woman." He bows his head to her in respect. "We should probably head to the caves if you want to get home."

Julia and Carmen nod as they follow behind him. The King leads them through a large garden that twists and turns into a maze of bushes. Julia's in awe at the flowers that entangle the bushes, vines all over them, even overhead, creating a luscious canopy. The colors are so vibrant it seems they are glowing. The King turns a corner, leading to a dead end. Carmen and Julia look at each other, confused. As they near the wall of shrubbery, King Rupert stops abruptly, turning to see the look of confusion on their faces. He swoops his hand to the side, pulling back the shrubs to reveal a small opening in a cave.

"This is the Cave of Secrets. Adventurers who enter can discover secrets or items lost to them. As easy as this sounds, I promise you it is not. You will be forced to face your own minds and challenged to leave behind something unexpected. You will be greeted by a goblin who will guide your way. DO NOT TOUCH HIM!" The King's words are sharp. Carmen and Julia look at each other with raised eyebrows.

"He can not touch you unless you touch him first. If you do, he will kill you. Goblins are hungry little monsters and will eat anything they touch. They have been cursed not to touch a living creature first. However, anyone who touches them voids the spell. Do I make myself clear?" The King lowers his head, becoming eye level with them. Julia and Carmen nod with nervousness. The King waves his free hand, pointing them to their way in. For a moment, neither move until Julia puts her hand on Carmen's back, pushing him to the opening. He stumbles forward, looking back at her.

"You're such a gentleman going first." Julia winks at him as he chuckles. Carmen smiles back before ducking into the cave. Julia ducks down, following after. The opening is a tight squeeze as they crouch to crawl in on their hands and knees. A few feet into the cave, it opens up, allowing them to stand and walk side by side. Carmen holds out his hand to Julia. She takes it moving forward with him. The cave goes on endlessly at a slight slope downwards. It's dark and damp, and Carmen holds a fireball for light. Neither of them speak as they peer into the darkness, looking for some hope that they will see what they need to see. Eventually, there is a dim light that gets brighter the closer they get. Carmen's flame goes out. He tries to reignite it but can't. He looks at Julia as she shrugs. With the light at the end growing bright, they just push on.

The sounds of rushing water in the distance echo around them. They can see a larger opening in the cave. At the edge of the opening, they stop dead in their tracks, mouths open in awe. It's a large cavern with a high ceiling, a small opening at the top, letting in light, and a small waterfall. It is surrounded by hanging grass. Near the waterfall is a large bush-like plant just hanging down. The path in front of them circles down the edges of the wall to a large basin full of grass and a few small trees. There is a pond filled with water from the waterfall above. In the middle of the opening is a large water fountain. As they descend, Julia points out that the fountain statue has three faces and six arms. Each arm holds a different object, all carved out of various types of stones.

"I really don't understand how this will help us get home. What are we looking for here?"

Carmen holds out a finger as he shushes her. He points to a tree in front of them. There's a strange figure peering from behind it. It has a green head shaped like a snake with long pointy ears. Its nose is flat to its face with just two long slits for openings. It smiles a large smile revealing rows of sharp, jagged teeth. Carmen crouches down, ready to fight.

"That must be the goblin we're looking for." Julia steps forward towards the creature. "Are you here to guide us? We really need to get home."

Carmen places a hand on her shoulder as a precaution. The goblin bolts from the tree, rushing to Julia. It crawls on all fours like a gorilla, letting out small grunts. Julia pulls back slightly.

"Ah, that I am. Take my hand, and I will lead the way for you. Hehe." The Goblin's voice is grainy and high-pitched. Julia cringes as it speaks. Slowly, it reaches out its long, lanky arm. Julia tries not to look disgusted as she studies its long fingers with long, dirty yellow fingernails.

"No, Thank you. I am alright. Please just lead the way." Julia shakes her head as she grabs Carmen's hand instead.

"Very well, hehe. I'm used to my offers of kindness getting rejected. Such a shame folks nowadays have no manners. hehe." The Goblin gives a big smile as it shakes its head. "Please proceed to the fountain and place your hands and feet on the placements. hehe." They make their way slowly to the fountain. The stones on the ground and top edge are worn down as if thousands of hands and feet have been in this spot before. They remove their shoes and nestle their feet in place. The Goblin creepily walks around them, still holding its smile. They look at it cautiously as it gestures to them to place their hands on the edge. Carmen clears his throat as he places his hands down, still holding eye contact. *"Very good. Now, look into the water and focus on your reflection. hehe."* Hesitantly, they glance down at the water and instantly fixate; the water draws them in. Although the fountain is running, there are no ripples. It's odd. Their reflections are clear and smooth. Their focus is now locked in, and neither notices the Goblin gently dipping a finger in front of their faces. As the ripples clear away their reflections, they are held in a trance, focusing on the water. Their faces slowly inch closer to it.

Carmen notices he can't see the bottom. There is no end to the fountain. He tries to pull back, but he can't. His face keeps inching closer and closer to the water involuntarily. He tries to yell and look over to Julia, but the water has him. He can't fight it. As the tip of his nose touches the water, he feels a surge of energy. Orange static surrounds his body as he gets sucked into the water. He gasps, taking in a breath. Now sinking into the bottomless pit of the fountain, Carmen regains control of his body. He tries swimming up, but the water is dragging him down. He looks up, and Julia is still looking into the water. He yells and waves his arms, letting out air bubbles, but she doesn't move. She is still locked in. Looking down, he can see a swirling arm of water wrapping around him, dragging him into the darkness. The only light remaining is the glow of the orange static around him. He remembers the static is always an indicator that he's on the right path. He stops struggling and lets it drag him down. He looks around to see if he can see anything, but the light isn't highlighting anything specific. He closes his eyes as he struggles to hold his breath. *When will this come to an end? How much longer will he need to hold his breath?* He could feel his body growing weak. He struggles to hold onto consciousness. His mouth falls open as the last of his air escapes his body, bubbling to the top.

Resurrection

J ulia tries to break her focus on the water. She feels it pulling her in. She screams for Carmen to help, but nothing comes out. She is helpless; she can't move. She needs to break her focus. Maybe if she can focus on hearing something, she can break away. She listens closely, knowing the Goblin has been walking around them, but there is nothing. She takes a deep breath in and focuses again. There is a splash next to her, and she can feel water hitting her face. She gasps as she sees Carmen dragged down, water swirling around him, pulling him down. The glow of his orange static lights him up clear as day. She tries to dive in after him to reach for him, but she is still locked in place. All she can do is watch him struggle. He goes further down, bubbles popping at the surface as he tries to break free. She sees tears well in her eyes as she watches the light fade as he sinks into the darkness. His struggle stops, along with bubbles of distress. She couldn't save him. She couldn't get him home. What is next? Is she going to suffer the same fate as Carmen? Is he the unexpected loss the King talked about? But what would be the point of the trial? This is all to help him get back home. She finally feels like she's found a family, a home. She finally feels love since the death of her parents. She loves Carmen. A tear drips from her nose. She watches it fall as if time is standing still. It glistens and shines from the light breaking through the cave's rooftop. As it breaks the water's surface, Julia feels a breeze rush around her body. It picks up, viciously whipping around her. She feels it pushing her body closer to the water. I guess it's my turn; she closes her eyes for a moment and feels the freedom as she stops fighting against the force dragging her under. She accepts death as her destiny. Wishing to join Carmen wherever he is. She thinks about Cypress; she will miss him, and he will surely miss her and Carmen. He will be alright, though; he found his father and a wonderful new home, and he will be loved and safe. With another gust of wind, Julia falls face-first into the water. She doesn't fight or struggle; she just lets the water drag her down as it did Carmen. She can feel it gently constrict around her body as she's pulled down. The light above fades quickly, leaving her in complete darkness.

She looks down to see if she can see Carmen's glow; she notices she's quickly heading toward a light that has appeared. *Hope fills her heart. Is this the end? Is Carmen still alive?* As she approaches the light, she closes her eyes and prepares for some impact. Her body leaves the water and free falls into the open air. Before she can open her eyes, she hits the ground. Oddly, it doesn't hurt. *Is she dead?* She slowly opens her eyes. She is in a large field with long grass. She looks around frantically; all she sees is a large bush and a waterfall. Curiously, she approaches them, something seems out of place. As she gets closer to the bush and the waterfall, she notices the light is coming from the water, and the water is flowing upwards. Slowly, she looks up and gasps, covering her mouth. Her head starts spinning as she crouches to the ground. Above her, she can see the fountain. She sees both her and Carmen still hunched over the water; the Goblin paces back and forth with its creepy smile. She falls back, clutching the grass in her fingers. Panic sets in, and she starts screaming for Carmen. He doesn't move, and the Goblin continues pacing unfazed. Her head spins as it tries to make sense of her new orientation. *How is she so grounded to the ceiling yet seeing her and Carmen on the ground?*

There is a faint whisper and rustling of branches coming from the bush. Slowly, she crawls her way over to it, too disoriented to stand. She reaches for the branches to pull them back, trying to reach the center. She sees something in there; it looks like a person. *"Carmen!"* She yells, pulling frantically at the branches. They are folded tight and are nearly impossible for her to pull back. She sinks back, giving the bush another look over. There has to be a way to get in there. Whatever she needs to look for has to be in this bush. The bush is dull green and brown as if it hasn't been getting any water, but it's still standing strong. She smells the branches and instantly pulls back. It gives off the most putrid smell.

"That's it!" Her eyes widen as she realizes what it is. It's an Anastatica Hierochuntica. She's only read about them and seen them in books; they are extremely rare. *"How did you*

get so big? Your species is only recorded to get the size of a pasta bowl." Julia studies the plant in amazement. She knows she needs to get water to the roots so it will open, but how? She slowly stands up, keeping her legs steady. Facing the waterfall, she holds out her hands and tries to move the water, as Carmen had once shown her. But nothing happens. Her powers don't work here. She quickly removes her belt and uses the metal buckle to dig into the earth around the bush. She extends the trench from the bush to the edge where the waterfall falls through. Quickly, she pulls at the bottom of one of her pant legs, ripping her pants open. She tears off a long piece of fabric. She anchors one end to the opening of her trench and stretches the other end out to touch the water. She smiles as water pours down her pant leg and fills the trench with water.

Quickly, the trench fills with water surrounding the bush. She pulls back, crawling over to it. She can see the bush sucking in water. Slowly, it becomes more vibrant, and all the brown disappears. She smiles pleasantly, surprised with herself. She can hear the branches creak as they try to open. Frantically, she pulls on them to help them open up.

"Carmen, I'm coming for you." The branches fling open, and Julia's mouth drops. She crawls up onto the open bush to the body in the middle. She lifts their head, tears streaming down her face as she holds their lifeless body heavy in her arms. "Why would you do this to me?" Julia screams out as the branches begin to rattle and shake. She falls back as the lifeless body lifts into the air. She hurries away from the bush. The branches begin emitting green orbs that shoot off surrounding the body, encasing it in light. Julia rubs the tears from her eyes trying to see better. Quickly, the bush dissipates as each part of it dissolves into little orbs to join the others. The body is now a ball of glowing light as it lowers to the ground. There is a massive gust of wind, and the orbs fly all over. Julia shields her face as she lowers her arms. Her face fills with joy, and tears rush down her cheeks.

"Why are you crying? You brought me back."

Julia runs over to hug her. *"Illiana, is it really you? How is this possible."* Julia's voice cracks as she squeezes her tight.

"Yes, it's me. The Cave of Secrets is powerful. It can make anything happen. The cave must have conjured me. What are you doing in the Cave of Secrets?"

Julia pulls back, confused. There is a coldness to Illiana's voice.

"If it can bring people back to life, wouldn't everyone come here to find their loved ones?"

Illiana just shakes her head.

"The King sent us in here. We must complete these tasks to get Carmen home." Julia continues. Illiana frowns.

"That stubborn dragon always has to overcomplicate things. You shouldn't be here; this place is too dangerous. While in here you can find something you lost or secrets you need to know, but you also lose something unexpected, which can be the same thing you find."

Julia lays her head on Illiana's chest. A tear escapes her eye. She's happy to have Illiana back but fears what may happen next. *"I can't lose you again. I will do anything to save you and bring you with us."*

Illiana pushes Julia back to meet her eyes. *"If it was that easy everyone would be venturing down here. These caves have tricky magic. The goblins control everything. They are nasty little bastards. We should find Carmen and get out of here."*

Julia lowers her brows for a moment studying Illiana's face. It's different. She seems so cold and distant. There is no light to her eyes and no jump in her voice. She shakes her head letting out a sigh as she points to the fountain. She needs to focus on getting back. She can't worry about Illiana until they are back to safety. Illiana nods as she walks to the waterfall. Julia tilts her head there isn't even the slightest bounce in her step. Even her walk is cold and empty. Julia shakes her head as she follows. She looks at the falls as the water rushes down to the fountain. *Are they really about to jump?* Julia's eyes widen as she looks down to where her physical body remains at the fountain, and shakes her head frantically.

Illiana lets out a sigh. "You won't get hurt. You are in an astral form; the only thing that can hurt you is the guardians, who can't enter the caves."

Julia nods as she slides her feet closer to the waterfall. She hesitates for a moment as she looks down. She can feel her heart beating a mile a minute. Slowly, she sticks her hand out to touch the water. She can feel it rushing hard over her hand. She looks back just as Illiana shoves her forward. Quickly, she shoots down the falls. With her eyes squeezed shut, she reaches out, hoping to grab her body. She feels her physical form hit the water as her astral form takes back over her body. She opens her eyes and falls backwards, rolling away from the fountain. She gets up quickly and rushes over to the fountain. She reaches in to help Illiana out. Julia reaches for Carmen as the Goblin shouts.

"DON'T TOUCH HIM!."

Julia pulls back quickly, snapping to look over at the Goblin. "If you move him in this state, he won't be able to get back to his body."

Julia looks at Illiana, who nods to confirm that what the Goblin says is true.

"I watched him drown. How do we help him?" Julia takes a deep breath, trying not to panic.

"He needs to figure this out for himself. The king should not have sent you here, especially ill-prepared."

Discovery

Carmen opens his eyes. He is sitting at the dining table across from his father. He looks around, confused. Julia is sitting beside him, and Cypress is at the other end. He smiles at her as she tilts her head, questioning his confusion.

"We made it home?" Carmen tries to sound excited. Julia giggles at him, shaking her head.

"Of course we did, my love, weeks ago. I know your memory has been bad since our arrival. You went into shock after you lost your hand going through the portal."

Carmen looks down at the bloody nub where his hand used to be. Carmen lets out a scream as he falls back in his chair. Julia jumps up to help him up. "It's okay, my love. We can go through this again. I know this isn't easy to hear, and it certainly doesn't get easier to tell." She guides him out of the dining hall. Carmen's heart is pounding out of his chest, his arms trembling.

"I don't understand. The last thing I remember is drowning in the fountain."

Julia shakes her head as she gently strokes his face.

"Love, you came back from the fountain talking about a door knob. It was all gibberish, to be honest. You had a door knob on you, and nothing made sense. It didn't even help us return home." Julia pulls a cloth from her pocket and unravels it in her lap. She holds up a gold door knob with the letter C on it. "I've been carrying it with me to help remind you of what happened. You told us something about it having a D and then changing to a C, but that's it. We have no idea what it means."

Carmen shakes his head as he reaches for it, forgetting his missing hand. Tears fall from his face as the realization hits him. Julia runs her fingers through his hair as she places the knob in his hand. He sits back fast as he sees the orange sparks connect his hand to the knob.

"You see that! The sparks mean we're on the right path!" Carmen looks up at Julia with hope in his eyes and a slight smile.

Only Julia isn't smiling back. "No, Carmen, I don't, I never did."

His smile fades, hearing the sadness in her voice.

Julia takes his hand in hers. "My love, you need to wake up."

Carmen tilts his head, confused. Julia gets up and walks back into the dining hall. Carmen sits there for a moment, trying to comprehend everything. Slowly, he gets up to rejoin his family. As he reaches for the doorknob, it falls to the floor. He watches it roll across the floor. He lifts his hand, studying the knob Julia had handed him. He rolls it in his fingers watching the sparks connect with it. Quickly he looks around before placing the knob in his hand in the spot where the original knob had fallen from. As he twists the knob, he hears the door click open. Pulling it open, he sees no light shining through. Peaking around the door, there is an open space with nothing. He hesitates for a moment until the orange sparks start flailing again. Cautiously, he steps into the door, trying to feel around for a floor. There is solid ground under his foot, but nothing to be seen. As he ventures in slowly, he leaves the door open for some light, hoping it will help him see something. There are footsteps in the distance; Carmen backs gradually to the door. As he backs up more and more, the footsteps get closer. He looks back, knowing he should have reached the door by now. All he can see is the dark, open space of night. Slowly, he takes in a deep breath, trying not to panic. He holds up his hands to form a fireball for some light, but nothing happens. He turns his hands over happily; he has both of them but is confused about why his powers won't work.

"Who's out there?" Carmen holds his hands out in front of him as he walks forward. He has to try to find his way out. "I can hear you walking. What do you want?" The footsteps stop as Carmen stops walking. He listens closely for a response.

"My boy, behind you."

Carmen turns around to see the same man from the door he found in the field at Dracfalls. He holds out his hand holding a ball of light.

"Do you know who I am?"

Carmen nods his head. "You are Domonic Remy."

Domonic smiles with a slight chuckle.

"Yes, But no. I mean, do you know who I am? Who I really am?"

Carmen shakes his head.

"Look a little closer, my boy. What do you notice?"

Carmen looks at him. He looks just like the portraits in the books he had read about him. Nothing seems familiar otherwise to him. He shakes his head again.

"You hold a great power that is like none other. It will take you and others to great places. You are a key to the outside. I once held these powers and now only live on as a memory inside these doors. I placed these memories in hopes you would one day find them." Domonic waves his hand, and 21 doors appear in a line. Carmen walks up to the doors. He recognizes most of them. Some are the ones held in his kingdom, and the others are those held in the other kingdoms. He runs his hand along them. With each one he touches, he hears murmurs coming from them as if he can hear their secrets.

"Can you teach me how to open them so I can go home?"

Domonic smiles, shaking his head.

"I wish I could, but I can not. From what I have discovered over my research, the power takes differently to each person it inhabits. All I can give you is to focus on where you need to be, not where you want to be. Feel the energy and let it take you away. Eventually, you can harness it and use it. I must urge you to be careful once you figure it out. As you probably already know, people are afraid of it and will kill you out of fear for their safety."

Carmen pulls his hand back from the doors and faces Domonic.

"I think I understand. I've read a lot about you and always felt like something was missing. I've recently been part of the tri-council for the three kingdoms, and they always discuss the importance of keeping the doors locked up. They never talk about why."

Domonic laughs as he shakes his head. "It's only misunderstood due to their ancestors' misuse of my powers. I opened the doors to help end world problems and bring comfort to people's lives. I discovered the king had secret armies going in at night, killing people and destroying villages, so we didn't know there was life in the doors. Little did they know I already knew this and had worked deals with the universes to share with us. I would regularly use my powers to help out in their struggling villages. I tried to stop the attack from happening, but the dragon king was so mad at what our people had done to them. His only promise was my family and I wouldn't get hurt. I did what I could to turn back time but couldn't undo what was already done; something was stopping me. Many were lost, and the people blamed me, not knowing what their own king had done to the people of these universes."

Carmen watches a tear fall from Domonics eye. He looks back at the doors, touching them once again. He moves his hand slowly, feeling the orange sparks dance.

"How can I change that though? Won't the same thing happen again?"

Domonic places his hand on Carmen's shoulder. He smiles big at him. Domonic looks down at his hand as he slowly begins to fade.

"I don't have much time left. I only gave myself a set amount of time at each door. But you are smart and strong. You are in a place of leadership; I was not. I am so thankful Deniha got out of the kingdom and birthed my beloved son Domonic Animus in a loving home. You will know what to do when the time is right. Remember to take your time and trust only those closest to you until you are ready. Let yourself learn first."

Domonic fades away with the doors, leaving Carmen alone in the darkness. He can feel his heart and mind swimming with all this new information. The name Domonic Animus rings in his mind. Everyone in the kingdom knows the story of King Domonic and his mother being found in the woods by King Alden. But the connection was never made. He kneels down on the ground to focus his mind. He takes several deep breaths to calm. Slowly, he sits down, crossing his legs to meditate.

"Okay, Where do I need to be? I am all yours; take me away." Carmen speaks the words as if he were speaking to another person. There is a tingle in his fingers as he speaks again. He can feel himself sinking into the floor with water surrounding him. He takes

a deep breath as he lets the feeling consume him. There is an unusual calmness about it. A reassurance that this is the right thing to let happen. As he sinks deeper and deeper, he doesn't let himself think about anything. He focuses on feeling the energy around him, trying to connect himself with it. The calmness and the comfort cradles his body as it carefully carries him away to wherever he needs to be. He keeps his eyes closed and lets his body stretch out as he drifts.

He feels his hands and knees touch down on a familiar cool stone surface. The sounds of the fountain reconnect him with his body. Slowly, he lifts his head, opening his eyes. A loud screech comes from behind him as Julia rushes to hug him tight. He turns to hug her and freezes. He smiles big as he sees Illiana sitting on a bench.

"Look who I found!" Julia's voice is light and joyful. Carmen smiles happy to see this side of her again. *"Did you find anything?"* Carmen nods as he hugs Julia tight. Illiana remains seated, disconnected from their joy.

They all turn when they hear a loud cackle. The Goblin races over, laughing maniacally.

"Such a sweet moment. Don't you love reunions? I know I do. Hehe. You know what else I love? I love payment. Hehe. Surely, you must have been warned."

"What do you want so we can leave?" Carmen turns, trying to tuck Julia behind him. The Goblin smugly looks around as it scratches its chin, thinking about what it wants. "Any day now, I want to go home."

"Chill, chill, my dear boy. You all took your time venturing, let me think. Hehe. I am very hungry, and you seem to have found me a tasty snack you didn't enter with. hehe." The Goblin licks its lips and eyes Illiana. "Or you can surrender the shinny shinny in your pocket. Gold really is my color. Hehe." Everyone begins patting their pockets. Carmen notices a lump in his pocket but tries to play it off as nothing. He has a faint idea of what it is. He keeps patting to play it off. The Goblin isn't fooled. It points a long green finger at him, smiling wide. "That's exactly what I am talking about. Hehe. Don't think you can fool me. I know everything that happens in these caves. Hehe." It stretches out its long arm, holding out its hand, waiting for its token. Carmen hesitantly steps forward, reaching into his pocket. His fingers come in contact with something metal. He feels the sparks shoot from his fingers. Slowly he pulls it from his pocket, revealing a gold door knob. On it is the letter D. There are no designs or anything else interesting about it. Sparks fly like crazy from Carmen's hand and the knob. The goblins' eyes light up with joy. *"Yes, this is what I require. Hehe. I can feel the power emanating off it."* Carmen extends his arm forward to surrender it. He has learned the secrets he needed to. *This simple door knob won't be that important, would it?* As Carmen places the knob in the Goblin's hand, it squeals loudly, making him jump. He feels his fingers brush the Goblin's hand, and its eyes open wide. Quickly, the Goblin jumps, grabbing Carmen's arm, pulling him in. Carmen struggles to get away, but the Goblin's grip is too strong. It takes a deep breath, smelling the side of Carmen's face. Julia lungs forward only to be pulled back by Illiana. *"My, my, very noble of you to offer yourself as a snack. It has been quite some time since I've eaten. Hehe."* It looks up at Julia and Illiana with a large smile. *"I would suggest you leave now.*

This is about to get real messy. Hehe." The Goblin bites into Carmen's shoulder.

Julia lets out a scream as Illiana tries dragging her to the pathway. Carmen clutches the knob in his hand as he jabs the narrow end into the Goblin's eye. Carmen falls to the ground, scrambling to the path with the others. The Goblin lunges high, landing on the pathway before them. Illiana grabs a rock, throwing it at the Goblin.

"You will give me my snack and leave. He is mine now, and there is nothing you can do to stop me." The Goblin breathes heavily, a black liquid oozing from its eye. Carmen tries to shape a fireball, but nothing happens. Carmen runs down the path towards the fountain with the Goblin following him. Illiana pulls Julia's arm as she drags her up the path.

"What are you doing? We can't just leave him here. He will die."

Illiana doesn't look back and just keeps moving. Julia doesn't pull against her. she's too focused on the empty expression on Illiana's face.

"If we can get to the top your powers will work again, you can call your book. There is a spell you can use to put him to sleep so we can get out."

Julia nods as she pushes on her feet to run with Illiana. At the top of the cave, Julia puts her hands on her knees, breathing hard. Illiana places a hand on her shoulder, trying to catch her breath as well. Carmen yells as he runs in circles from the Goblin down below.

"Quick, call the book. It's connected to your powers and will respond if you call it."

Julia nods as she closes her eyes and envisions the book. She holds her palms upwards to catch it. She tries to feel its energy, but it isn't coming to her. She clenches her fist in frustration. She can't focus with the squeals of the Goblin and Carmen. She covers her ears and crouches down. She feels Illiana's hand on her shoulders. She takes a deep breath and tries envisioning the book again. There is a ringing in her ears, and her hands tremble.

Frustration takes over, and she jumps up, pushing Illiana to the side. She takes a deep breath and leans forward, sending a sonic scream into the Cavern. The Goblin and Carmen fly across the Cavern, slamming into the rock wall. Quickly, it launches off the wall, climbing to Julia. She screams again, this time holding the scream, pinning the Goblin to the floor of the Cavern. Carmen stumbles to his feet as he races up the path. The Goblin twitches and flails as it tries to peel its body away from the ground it's being forced against. At the top of the path, Carmen steps out of the cave. He sticks out his hands, twisting his wrist from side to side. The rock around the opening to the cave starts closing up. Julia stops screaming as she tries to catch her breath. Carmen grabs her arm, pulling her through the cave. The three-run as fast as they can. The Goblin is strong, and they don't know if the cave wall will hold it for long. They run faster and faster as they see the light guiding them to the end of the cave for safety. Carmen jumps, pulling Julia through the opening with him. They roll on the ground, stopping at the king's feet. He looks down with a big smile.

"Well, Well, Well, I see you made it out alive but barely. I will take you to the infirmary before we move on to your next test. I hope you learned what you needed to do while in there."

Carmen covers his face, wincing as he realizes the pain in his shoulder for the first time. Illiana drops to the ground next to them, panting out of breath. Julia places a hand over Carmen's shoulder; she hums lightly, and her hand begins to glow.

"You can try all you want, but that won't work. Goblin bites are a little more complicated than that. Their saliva is often collected to fight against magic as it has impervious properties."

Julia drops her hand down and sighs. Carmen pets her hand as he gives her a thankful smile.

There's a loud squeal as Illiana yells. Everyone looks over to Cypress, jumping at Illiana. His mouth open, and his tongue flopping out the side. He lands on her with a hard thud.

"Get off of me! You're getting me wet with your slobber!" She pushes his face away, wiggling herself out from under him. Cypress pulls back whimpering with confusion as he hides behind the King. The King laughs, ushering everyone out of the garden.

"Illiana, It's good to see you again. You were right about these two. They sure are something special." Illiana waves a hand at him with annoyance as he turns to walk away.

Julia jumps to her feet to help Carmen, trying not to put pressure on his shoulder. He looks at Julia confused as he gestures towards Illiana.

Julia shrugs as she pulls him in for a hug. "Something is wrong with her. It's like she's just an empty shell with no emotions." Just as the words slip from her mouth her eyes widen. "She has no emotions because I have them. When she gave me her life force at the swamp everything was transferred to me. When she came back she didn't come back with emotions because I still have them." Julia runs forward pulling Carmen with her, to catch up with the rest. Carmen winces as the pain surges through his shoulder.

Internal Battle

Carmen winces as the nurse stitches up his arm. She smiles at him caringly and is careful with each stitch. Julia watches her closely. She notices the nurse's hands unnecessarily brushing over Carmen's chest and arms. She takes a deep breath to hide her growing annoyance.

"I'm so sorry I couldn't heal you; if you had been bitten by anything else, I would have been able to help you. That goblin bite is something else. Illiana told me they have oils in their saliva that magic can't touch." Julia glares at the nurse as she rubs down his arm.

"My beautiful, don't beat yourself up over something no magic can fix," Carmen says, looking at Julia.

The nurse giggles at him as she keeps stitching. "You know you're being so brave right now. I know I would be in so much pain crying if I were bit by a goblin." She bats her eyelashes at him with a big smile. Julia rolls her eyes as her face turns red with anger. "I can't believe you made it out alive. You are so strong; you can probably make it out of anything." Her hands brush over Carmen's biceps again, and Julia groans loudly.

"How about you just focus on stitching him up rather than flirting with him." Both Carmen and the nurse look at her with wide eyes. Just as the nurse goes to speak, Julia throws up her arms and storms off. Carmen chuckles as the nurse shoots daggers at him, her face red with anger. Carmen shrugs, and she jabs the needle into his arm hard; he lets out a little screech as he winces. He sighs, knowing she is done being gentle with him.

Once stitched up, the nurse gets up and leaves without a word. Carmen carefully pulls his shirt over his head and bolts out of the room. He makes his way through the halls to Julia's room. He smiles, finding cuteness in her jealousy. He pushes her door open slowly. There she is, perched in the window, studying her spell book. Her red hair is down over her shoulders, glowing in the sunlight. She hadn't noticed him enter the room. He watches her for a while. Admiring her beauty.

"I hope you know jealousy looks kind of cute on you, but you can't flip out on every girl that talks to me." Carmen places an arm on the doorway and leans into it. With his head tilted slightly, he raises an eyebrow at her. She turns to look at him slowly. Her head is still lowered as if she were still reading, causing her hair to fall over her eyes. She cracks a smile at him mischievously.

"Oh, really now. Well, I didn't grow up with a family, so I didn't learn how to share with others, and that's not going to start now." She raises an eyebrow at him as she leans back in the window. Carmen hangs his head down as he chuckles to himself.

"So what are you looking into? Anything interesting?" Carmen points to the spell book in her lap as he strolls over. Julia rolls her eyes and sighs as she flips to the next page.

"When Illiana gave her life for me. In doing so, she gave me her powers, along with most of her memories. She's the King's visionary, and they still need her. I am looking for a way to give them back or share some of my powers with her so she can continue her work, as it seems her powers didn't return to her when she was brought back."

Carmen wraps his arms around her, kissing the top of her head.

"I just got her back, and I'm gonna have to leave her behind." Julia sighs as she tilts her head into Carmen's chest.

"I know it's hard, but her whole life has been here. She has a family and a duty to her people. She can't just up and leave for a whole new universe."

Julia sighs and looks at him, annoyed. Carmen pulls back, holding his hands up.

"Yeah, well, they moved on just fine when she was dead. Plus, I brought her back to life in the cave of secrets because she was what I lost, so her path with us shouldn't be over yet." Julia screams in sadness while punching Carmen's bad shoulder in frustration. He winces, gritting his teeth to hide his pain.

"Yes, that is true, but maybe the caves brought her back to give you back self-confidence. You were full of love, joy, and independence when we first met. You were strong-willed; you could do anything you wanted. Over the last couple of days, you've become angry with the world and scared. Even *though you have the right to be, it's not who you are."*

Julia gives him a half smile before scowling at him and punching him in the arm again.

"What is wrong with you? You're gonna rip my stitches."

It was nice to have what I thought was a family to help me and let me feel a bit of vulnerability for once in my life! Maybe feeling a bit scared of losing you, her, and Cypress is nice because I don't want to be alone anymore and do it all alone! Now get out of my room!" Julia raises her voice with each word as she pokes at Carmen's chest. *"GET OUT! GET OUT! GET OUT!"* Julia slams the door in his face. She leans against the door to hold it shut as tears stream down her face. Carmen knocks gently on the door. *"Just please go. The king is probably waiting for us in the gardens. I will be out; I just need a minute to myself."*

Carmen leans his head against the door and whispers.

"You'll never lose me. I'll always be here." He pauses momentarily before pulling back and ventures down the hall. Julia sobs as she wipes

away the tears from her eyes and nose. She feels a pit in her stomach. Carmen didn't deserve her out-lash. It isn't his fault. He's only trying to make her feel better. She hits her head against the door. How could she push him away like that? She wants him close, but she just keeps pushing him away. Julia wonders if part of her emotional outburst is from having Illianas feelings inside her. She can feel the loss of Illiana's home and the struggles with her family. Could her fears just be amplifying Julia's fears? Julia forces herself up and out the door. She just wants to be held in Carmen's arms. It makes her feel warm and safe.

She walks quickly out the back of the castle doors and into the field. She slows as she nears the opening of the gardens. Everyone is there; the King, Carmen, Cypress, and even Illiana are waving happily at her. She stops and takes a deep breath. At first glance, anger flashes over her, and she inhales deeply to calm herself. Then she realizes Carmen is right; she does have a life here; she can't just expect her to leave everything behind. Memories flash of Illiana with the King and helping the villagers. Memories of her celebrating with her family and friends. Memories of her with an old boyfriend. She was happy as they looked at new cabins together. She musters up a small smile and waves back. She needs to find a balance between all her feelings and emotions. She needs to find a way to separate Illianas from her own. She searches the group and gives Carmen a hug while muttering sorry to him. Carmen reassuringly kisses the top of her head, and everything melts away. The king clears his throat, and Julia brings her focus to him.

"If you don't mind, I'd like to begin now; we don't have all day. I would like to get you home by nightfall."

Julia nods as she pulls back, leaving an arm around Carmen's waist. She sinks into his side and smiles.

He is warm.

He is comfy.

He is home.

Her focus snaps back to the king as he continues speaking. *"Your next challenge is in the forest on the back side of the gardens. You must discover the ancestor and ask her for guidance. If she agrees to help you, she will show you her ways. However, if she does not agree to help you, she will not let you leave the forest alive. Julia, this task is for Carmen and Carmen alone. You will stay here with Cypress and I."*

Julia looks up at Carmen, shaking her head. She doesn't want to leave his side. *"I want to go with him, I'm not staying."* She stomps her foot to hold her ground. The King charges forward at her, lowering his head to her level. She holds firm and doesn't back down.

"This is not optional. Your death will be guaranteed if you enter. Only one may enter at a time. If the ancestor feels threatened, she will kill everyone. DO I MAKE MYSELF CLEAR!" He snorts a small puff of smoke in her face. She doesn't move for a moment; she holds her gaze and stands her ground. Carmen rubs the side of her arm to let her know he will be alright. Without looking at him, she nods and steps back. Illiana grabs her arm, pulling her in for a side hug. *"Good, it's settled then. Carmen, you may enter now; good luck to you."*

The Ancestor

Carmen makes his way through the garden. He glides his hand along the walls of shrubs, letting orange sparks fly about, guiding him. At the back of the garden, there's a viney opening just like the Cave. Carmen pulls back the branches to enter. Inside is not the forest he expected. The shrub walls create mazes that surround a big open area. Nothing but a single tree resides in the otherwise vacant space. Its top is large and full of green leaves that block out any light from coming in. Carmen approaches slowly, a little confused. Vines drape down from the tree branches. The large tree roots weave through the area in and out of the ground. He reaches forward to touch one of the protruding roots as he ducks under it. As his fingers touch the smooth wood, orange static shoots from his fingers and travels down to the roots. He pulls his hand back instantly. Light begins twinkling around him; the orange glow quickly runs through the branches and leaves before fading. Slowly, he reaches forward, keeping hold of the root. A continuous stream of orange flows from his fingers, spreading through the tree. The orange glow begins to change as it spreads, causing a rainbow of colors to twinkle throughout. Its branches and leaves fill with colorful light. Amazingly, he climbs through the roots to get closer to the trunk. He's amazed, watching all the colors flow throughout the more he touches it. Carmen spins around, trying to look at everything. Although confused, he smiles big, feeling more alive and connected than he's ever felt in his life. Carmen feels like he can feel the whole world in his hands.

"Isn't it wonderful the bond between universes that can be made?"

Carmen falls back, looking around for the voice. It's loud and rough. It doesn't sound like just one person speaking but many in unison. *"Child, don't be scared. I will not harm you. I am Life and Death; I am the bridge between all universes. A small piece of me lives on all planes. Some call me the Ancient one or the Ancestor, but my name is*

Lignum Vitae. I have visitors of all kinds, but rarely can they hear me speak."

Carmen props himself up. The branches begin to rustle, and the roots start to shake. The root lifts from the ground, raising Carmen closer to the tree top. His hands grip the root to steady himself from falling.

"I was told you would be able to provide me guidance. I am trying to get home. I don't belong in this universe."

The rattling of the tree intensifies as she laughs at Carmen.

"Did I say something funny?"

"My child, you are right where you need to be. You belong where you are needed. Your ancestor Domonic once visited me on many planes, always struggling to understand what he was destined to do. His heart was too kind and pure to accomplish what I intended. He had more power than he could ever imagine, but he also believed that he could change the world completely for the better rather than mold it to be what is needed. My child, you chose to see the power flowing and moving.

I've seen the great things you will do when ready."

"Does this mean I can travel like Domonic could? Do I have the power to travel as he did? How am I choosing to see the power? It just happens." Carmen smiles, hoping he's finally starting to understand his strange powers and all the strange things that have happened to him. The tree lets out another hearty laugh.

"Traveling is the simplest form of your power, my child. You are so much more than that. You are the positive and negative force of energy. You can take what you need but also give to those in need. You are a light to those walking the darkest of paths. You are the darkness to those who bask in the light, casting their shadows upon the unsuspecting. Carmen, you are the gray area of the world."

Carmen looks down at his hands. He touches the root under him. He watches his glow travel around the tree, lighting the leaves and branches. He takes a breath as his mind follows its movements. He smiles as he feels his own energy flowing through the tree and the energy of the tree pulling him in.

"So this glow is my guidance? Will it help me to learn and grow?"

"If you listen to it, yes. You can also use it. It is the energy I planted in your bloodline eternities ago."

A tear rolls from Carmen's eyes as he is engulfed in beauty and knowledge. He's beginning to see things. He can see all his ancestors from before him. He can see their successes and failures. Carmen wonders if they had all experienced what he is now. Then, the realization strikes him; he's still blind to so much information. Things have only been coming to him in bits and pieces. Knowledge only comes to him in random spurts. He can't pull this info whenever he wants to.

"Why couldn't I see it before if I've always had it? I read that Domonic used his powers at a young age. I've tried to figure it out, but it comes to me randomly. I can't recreate anything."

"My child, it has always been within you, waiting for you to be willing to see it. You can have all the knowledge and want to do it, but you need the willingness to accept the information. My power flowing through you knows what you need when you need it. when you are willing, it lets you have it. Do not rush things, Carmen. Take your time, experience life, and explore options. You can't be too kind or act impulsively, or bad things will happen."

"How can I learn more?"

"You learn over time, my child. You need patience and understanding. You have a small understanding now, and things will come to you a little more naturally. Grow from there, and you will flourish."

Carmen lays in the grove of the root. He rubs both hands on the roots to his sides and watches as the colors flash and spread through the tree. His eyes dance as his body falls into a trance. He can feel the energy of life flowing through the tree, connecting with the energy flowing from his hands. He feels like he is becoming one with the tree. The branches blend together, and he sees the universes coming together. He feels the push and pull of their energies. The murmurs of life flood his ears. He listens closely to see if he can hear his father's voice. Carmen tries to see if his father is looking for him. He wonders if his father has noticed he's missing. A woman's voice echoes softly, catching his attention.

"Darling, I'm here with you. I have always been with you. Darling, can you hear me?"

Carmen sits up, looking around frantically. There's nothing else here, but the voice calling out to him is clear in the sea of noise.

"Who are you? Where are you?" Carmen tries focusing on the voice in the sea of voices. He lays back again, gently brushing his hand along the wood of the roots. He can still hear her voice, but it's softer now; he can't make out the words. Carmen sits back up, looking at the tree trunk. "Who was that? Who was speaking to me?"

"Those who have passed on are still here; their energies never fade. Some chose to try *another life, and some want to stick around to watch loved ones grow."*

Carmen's eyes widen as another tear rolls down his face. Smiling, he leans back.

"I never met my mother, but my father told me she was always with me."

"My child, he was correct; she has always been with you. She's waiting for her time to rejoin you, as everyone else does. Do you understand why you are here? Do you know what you need to do for now?"

Carmen takes a deep breath and presses his fingers against the wood of the roots. He takes another breath, exhaling gently and focusing more on the energy. His orange glow transitions from orange to red, then to purple. The colors dancing through the leaves changing their color as well. He sees the shape of a woman forming in the colors. She smiles while blowing him a kiss. He mouths the words mom as tears roll down his cheek. Slowly, she points to another section of the tree top. He can see himself kneeling on the ground. The feeling of weakness runs through him. A figure approaches him, placing a hand on his shoulder. Strength returns to him, and the images fade, changing to a sea of colors twinkling about.

"I'm starting to, I don't understand everything, but I know I will. Thank you for your guidance."

The tree rattles and shakes again. The roots descend, bringing him back to the ground. He stands, being sure to keep his hands on the roots.

"My child, If you ever need me again, you can find me no matter what universe you're in. I will be there."

Carmen bows to the tree; he pulls his hand from the root to return to the garden. He watches the last colors twinkle and fade before letting the vines drop to block his view.

He hurries through the garden, rushing his way to Julia. He runs straight to her, stopping abruptly in front of her and holds her hands. She smiles as she slowly reaches her hand to him. Gently, she touches the palm of his hand with her fingertips, the orange static dancing between them. He moves his hand past her wrist and up her arms, the static following his fingers as he goes. Reaching her cheek, he gently grips her chin, pulling her in for a kiss, the static bouncing frantically between them. Cypress lets out a loud groan as he covers his eyes. Julia laughs as she pulls back. A smile stretches across her face. Carmen doesn't move his hand from her face for a long moment, stroking his finger slowly back and forth across her cheek as he feels his energy connecting with hers. The orange glow turns to pink, then red. Julia's eyes widen as she feels the warmth grow against her face. Her eyes close as she leans into his hands. Carmen places his head against hers as he whispers softly.

"Strength comes from the heart, and you hold mine. I was weak because I needed to find you. This was our destiny all along."

The Split

Night has fallen, and the moon shines bright above. Illiana wanders off from the others celebrating Hugh and his brother's birthday, to which neither attended. King Rupert is working to prepare Carmen and Julia's next task. Carmen and Cypress dance around the fire as a band plays. Butlers walk around with platters of food and drinks. Julia slips away, following Illiana to see what she is up to. She stays hidden as she follows; Illiana keeps checking to ensure no one is tailing her. She goes into the greenhouse on the south side of the castle. She doesn't light any of the lights; she just lurks in the darkness.

Julia ducks down as she approaches the glass building. She pokes her head up slightly to see inside. It's hard to see inside with the bright glow of the fire behind her reflecting on the glass. She crab walks along the glass to the backside, hoping not to be seen. She opens the door and slips in carefully, being sure to stay low. Although dark, the moon lights the inside well. The walls are cluttered with plants of all kinds; several planters hang from the rafters, vining all over the place. It's peaceful and quiet. Julia ducks back against a workbench as a shadow rises over her. Illiana is dragging a large birdbath to the center of the room. She keeps turning it as if trying to find a specific position. She keeps *hmmm'ing* and *mhm'ing* to herself until she gives a final *ah ha!* She fills it with water and fixes two large candles to the sides.

"If you're gonna stalk me, you could at least help me." Illiana's voice is cold and harsh as she continues setting up.

Julia stands up, startled, banging her head on the workbench. She begins to stutter.

"I may not have my powers, but I can still use my divination tools. I knew you would follow me here."

Julia walks over, rubbing her head. She reaches out, snapping her fingers and lighting the candles.

"Hmmm, About time you get the hang of it."
She turns to Julia, who is letting out a sad sigh.

"Well, it's easy when I have all the knowledge from the Covens book, and your memories, and emotions." She breathes deeply trying to remember Illiana's actions are only coming off as rude due to her emotionless state. "It's so hard to sort out my emotions from yours, and I feel like I'm pushing everyone away." Julia takes Illiana's hand as she pulls her closer.

"It was the only way I could save you. I set out to protect you and Carmen, and then you died on me. I had to do whatever I could to bring you back and give you a fighting chance."

Julia drops her head, trying to hold back tears. Illiana hooks a finger under her chin, lifting her head back up. "I can help you remove them, but I need you to trust me and do as I say."

Julia nods. "I would like to share my powers with you. I know you need them to continue working for the Kings; I just couldn't find anything in my book." Julia confesses.

Illiana stares blankly at Julia. "They already replaced me. They can not move on comfortably without guidance from a visionary. I am only here at the castle until I can pack my things."

Julia drops her head again, only for Illiana to pull it back up.

"I need you to stop being soft on me and focus. I will be alright, that just means I am on a new path. A path that I can choose. Maybe a path with my new family."

Julia's eyes light up with joy. Although cold and empty Illianas words feel hopeful and honest. "What about your family here? Won't you miss them?"

Illiana shakes her head. "Once Carmen can successfully unlock his potential, which will be tonight. We can come visit anytime we want."

Julia scrunches her eyebrows, tilting her head with confusion.

"Carmen is the key to the universe. He can open the doors anytime. He just doesn't know it yet. The kingdom is sending me with him to ensure his success."

Julia remains confused. *Does Carmen know this? Did he get these powers from the ancestor or did he always have them? If he does know, why aren't they already on their way to his universe so he can get home to his family and the village?* He hasn't discussed it since he exited the garden from his last task. She can feel something different about his energy and confidence but hasn't asked him about it. She is overwhelmed with questions and doesn't know what to say. She pushes them all to the back of her mind and tries to focus on the current moment.

"Okay, how do we remove these memories and emotions and give you some powers back."

Illiana holds out a hand to stop her.

"One step at a time, let's remove the memories and emotions. The powers will have to be sorted out another day. I am in no rush to get them back."

Julia nods in agreement. They sit opposite each other with the birdbath between them.

"I will send you to the astral plane again, just like you were in the caves, but this time, I want you to find me there and lead me to the water. This will be the side of me that split from me and lives within you. Now place your hands on the edge of the bath, letting your fingers dip in the water. Focus on your reflection."

Julia nods as she sits forward, looking into the water. It's cold on her fingers. She feels a string of fear run down her back as she remembers her experience in the cave. A single tear drips from her eye, creating ripples in the water. She feels her face drawing towards it. She panics and tries pulling back, but it's too late. Her body is heavy as it sinks closer and closer to the water. As her nose touches the water, she falls into it. She closes her eyes as she feels her body twist and fall until she falls back, hitting the ground. Did she pull herself out of the trance?

"I'm so sorry I got scared. I can try again." There's no response from Illiana. Julia looks up while pulling herself to her feet. She freezes for a moment, holding onto the bath, and watches herself and Illiana stand there motionless. She did it! But how is she going to find Illiana? She looks around and sees nothing but plants and more plants. Maybe she's in another part of the castle. She heads for the door, but it vanishes as she goes to push on it. She looks outside the glass to call for help, but there's no one around. The fire is the only thing blazing. *Where did everyone go? Why would everyone have left the party? They wouldn't have!* Julia turns back to see her and Illiana still hunched over the bath. *Why is she still seeing Illiana if she can't see anyone else?* She walks over cautiously. Watching the imposter.

"How do I remove you? I need my headspace back so I can think clearly." Julia speaks to Illiana with no response; she stands motionless. "Speak to me. I know you're not her!" Illiana sighs with a smile.

"But dear, I am a part of you. Don't you want me to be part of your family? We can be close forever. We can be forever bonded!" Illianas eyes are wide, unblinking. She smiles unnaturally wide. *"Do you not want me to be part of your life?"* Still unchanged, her eyes begin to leak tears. Julia approaches slowly.

"I do, I really do. But this is not how I want to do this. I still need to be my own person. You need to be your own person."

Illiana lunges at her, pushing her to the ground. Julia wiggles her feet up, kicking her off. Illiana gets up, her face filled with rage, and her eyes are still wide. She lunges for Julia again, but this time, Julia ducks to the side, sticking her foot out to trip her.

"This is not you. Why are you doing this?" Julia yells loudly. She sticks her hand out, trying to move the earth to hold her down, but nothing happens. Illiana laughs maniacally.

"Your powers don't work here." She lunges again, pushing Julia against the bath. She pushes her head into the water, trying to submerge her face. "If we can't be one, I'll take you out, and it can just be me!" She laughs uncontrollably.

Julia kicks and screams, trying to fight back. Her mouth fills with water with every gasp. She closes her eyes to try and calm her mind. She needs to wake up or think of a way out of this. Illiana pushes harder and harder on her head. White spots begin flashing behind her eyelids. She tries to take a breath to calm herself, only to suck in water and choke. Clenching her fist, she kicks her leg, hoping to aim for Illiana's ankle. She remembers a memory of Illiana getting picked on for weak ankles. It's one of the many terrible memories that keep her awake at night. She feels herself make contact. Illianas grip loosens on her head. She's able to pull out of the water and put Illiana's face under in her place. She stands on Illiana's ankle making her scream out. Tears flood her face as she drowns someone she loves. She pushes harder knowing this is the right thing to do. She reminds herself that Illiana is only fighting back in fear. If she could rid herself of all her trauma, her negative thoughts, and memories she wouldn't want to go back either.

"Illiana, please stop fighting me. I know you're scared but the bad memories and experiences are what makes you the wonderful amazing person you are. The person I love." Julia cries more with each word pouring out her mouth. Illiana's struggle slows as she relaxes in the bowl. Julia lightens her grip.

"Come back now. Come back to me."

Julia hears Illianas's voice beckoning her. She leans forward, dipping her head into the water as well. Instantly, she can feel her body falling. In the darkness, she flails to find some sort of stability until her body hits the ground. Illiana lifts her up, cradling her in her arms. Julia sobs louder and louder.

"You did it. You are alright. Stop whining"

Julia lifts her head angrily. Illiana shakes her head as she points to the bowl.

"Come look, you're free." She helps Julia up and leads her to the bowl.

At first, Julia hesitates. She leans forward, noticing a white and pink swirl in the water. *"Is that you?"*

Illiana nods.

"What do we do now?"

Illiana gets a jar from the workbench and dips it in the water, scooping it up. Slowly, she brings it to her mouth, and with three big gulps, she drinks it.

"Gezz, at least you got the easy part." Julia smiles at her, finally feeling free in her own mind.

Illiana chokes a little as she starts to laugh. *"I guess I did, my dear. I am so sorry you had to deal with my trauma."*

Julia shakes her head. Julia pulls her in for a hug. Tears roll down Julias face as she feels her hug back. A smile stretches across her face hearing the emotion in her voice again. *"No, I am sorry for all you've been through. I know it's hard but I don't know how you managed to hold yourself together. I know I couldn't."*

Illiana laughs. *"Because I see it as a blessing, my dear."*

Julia shakes her head, raising her eyebrows.

"Through all the bad I've endured, it has made me the person I am today, and life has given me the opportunity time and time again to do the right things. I am blessed with everything I have survived." Illiana winks as she rephrases Julia's words.

Julia hugs her tighter. *"I am blessed with such a wonderful Mum."*

Illiana freezes for a moment. She's overwhelmed with sadness and joy all at once. She sobs as emotions flood her once again. She had been deprived of the one thing she always wanted in life, and Julia is giving her that honor. She leans into her hug. Tears dripping down her face.

"Thank you, my dear, I am forever grateful."

The First of Many

J ulia runs over to Carmen, who is still dancing by the fire. She jumps into his arms, hugging him tight around the neck and pulling him into a kiss.

"Everything alright?" Carmen asks with a little chuckle in his voice. Julia leans back nodding with a big smile. She leans in, kissing him again. Nothing else matters in this moment. She even blocks out Cypress' squeals of disgust. For the first time since she started falling for him, she feels she can truly enjoy him with a clear mind all her own.

King Rupert interrupts everyone with a loud roar. Carmen places her on the ground as he approaches them. Everyone else at the celebration stops. The music ends abruptly, and all focus is on them.

"You have been through a great journey. I have tested not only your being but also your true intentions. Many keys have been before you, but they have all brought us trouble and terror. You will be the strongest key of them all. I needed to be sure you wouldn't be the end of our universe before I decided if you live or die. I have spoken with the great Lignum Vitae, and they are certain you will bring greatness to all the universes when the time comes."

Everyone cheers and claps. Carmen's face turns red; even being a prince, he has never before received such recognition.

"How can they be certain I will do the right thing? I have no idea how to even use my abilities." He looks around at all the smiling faces. Fear starts setting in as the realization comes to him. Being Animus' future king he knows people will depend on him to do the right thing and he is ready. Now the weight of people in another universe depending on him makes him wonder if he is truly ready. What life is there on the other universes and will they be depending on him as well?

King Rupert smiles as he lowers his head. "You will learn quickly now that you have unlocked what you need to know. But Lignum Vitae is the beginning and end of everything we know, see, hear, and feel. They are the creator and destroyer. If you weren't true of heart, they would have killed you before you got a chance to even enter their space." King Rupert raises his head again to speak louder. *"With that being said. My promise to you."*

King Rpuert turns to the open field. The group of people standing there scatter from the area. He pulls his head back, taking in a deep breath. With a loud roar, he extends his head forward. Opening his mouth wide, purple fire shoots from his mouth, striking the ground in the field. He pulls back his head again, taking in a bigger breath. He flings his head forward with another loud roar, shooting more purple fire. The blaze is mesmerizing, and everyone yells and cheers as it burns. The purple color slowly fades to a deep red, getting progressively lighter, slowly fading to orange and yellow. The king pulls back his head one last time, inhaling all the air he possibly can. Throwing his head forward, he blows a big gust of air at the flame, extinguishing it. Smoke fills the air as everyone's cheers turn to coughs for air. As the smoke clears, there are only gasps of confusion.

"I don't understand what this is!" Carmen yells with confusion. He expected to

see a portal home, yet all that is there is a door. The king waves his arms at the door for him to take a closer look. Hesitantly, he steps forward. His eyes widen when he realizes it's the same door he had fallen into to get here.

"I can only send and retrieve people and things from places within our universe, not out. So I present to you the door to your home."

Carmen shakes his head. "I don't know how to use my powers yet." He looks at the door again seeing it's missing a door knob. "I don't even have a door kn-" Carmen pauses for a moment. He reaches into his pocket and pulls out the door knob he received in the Cave of Secrets. It glistens from the fire burning behind him. He studies the D on it. Domonic was the last person to bring the doors alive. *Would he be able to do the same?* There's a low murmur as Carmen approaches the door. Slowly he holds out the knob to place it into the hole where it belongs. Orange static connects between the knob and the door. Carmen hesitates for a moment before the knob shoots out of his hand, placing itself in the door. The orange glow runs around the inside edge of the door, then shoots back at Carmen, throwing him back. Julia runs to his side to help him up. They both focus on the door watching the orange glow fade. Carmen's heart races as he presses forward. He grabs the knob, turning it slowly. There's a loud click, and he pushes on the door. It creeks loudly and gasps are heard as everyone gazes into the black and purple vortex. Julia grabs Carmen's hand, squeezing it tight. Carmen turns back. *"Thank you, sir. I am grateful for you."*

King Rupert nods, bowing his head. *"You are welcome. I pray you care for my son and my visionary and let them visit occasionally once your powers are stronger."*

Carmen and Julia's eyes widen. Cypress jumps with joy, squealing. Across the field, they can hear Illiana yelling at them.

"Wait for me! Wait for me! Please don't leave me behind dears."

Julia laughs as she watches her stumble across the field with bags in hand. She has four large cases tucked under her arms as she runs. Carmen grabs two of her bags to help her out.

"But Sir Cypress belongs with his father."

Cypress rubs his head against Carmen's hand, showing him pieces of the conversation with his father he had left out. Carmen and King Rupert nod to each other with understanding.

"I know he will be safer in the hands of his family. I also know you're going to let my boy visit me." The king bows his head, raising a thick, scaly eyebrow at Carmen. He smiles as he pets Cypress on the head.

Everyone grabs hands as they face the open door.

"Well, I guess this is it. Let's go home."

Cypress squeals as he darts through the door, vanishing into the vortex. Julia bolts after him, pulling Carmen and Illiana with her. As they pass through the doorway, everything comes into view.

Note from the Author!

Thank you to everyone who has read the book. I hope you enjoyed it and are looking forward to the next book coming to you soon. I appreciate your support!

Continue the journey with Carmen and Julia in 2026!

SNEAK PEAK

on the next page

Carmen's Destiny

Taking the Unexpected Path

By DJ Bajraktari

Home Sweet Home?

Julia and Illiana look around at the other doors laid out. Illiana walks around, running her hand along them. Cypress jumps around happily, squealing. The door slams shut behind them, and everyone turns.

"Welcome home, everyone. We need to find a way to get Cypress to the castle without being seen. We don't have dragons here."

Cypress skids to a stop, perking up his ears. His head lowers as he whimpers.

"Buddy, it's ok. My dad and uncle will love you. The guards will love you once they know you; I just don't want them to attack you if they mistake you for a threat."

Illiana holds up a finger and starts digging through one of her bags. Julia crouches over by Cypress to pet him on the head. He rubs his head against her with a low purr. Illiana rips a book from the bag and holds it up. It is Julia's spell book.

"There is a spell in here that you can use to make Cypress invisible for a short while. Hopefully it will last long enough for us to get into the castle."

Julia runs over, grabbing the book to read through it. Carmen goes over to open the door to the monument to make sure no one is standing watch. He hadn't thought of someone being there until just now. Unlike in their previous time frame, the sun was shining brightly. He peers around the door. No one is in sight, and the ground is wet from the fresh rain. The guards must have gone into the building while it rained.

"Ahha!" Julia jumps up, pointing a finger at Cypress. "Reflexion," Julia's finger lights up. She waves it at Cypress, and the light shoots out, hitting his arm. He jumps around, scared, as he starts to fade away. "Cypress, calm down, buddy. We need you to stay quiet for a little bit. I can keep you hidden if I hold my hand pointing at you."

Cypress lowers his head to the ground, letting out a whimper. Illiana walks over, feeling around to pet his head.

"My dear, I'll hold onto you while we walk if that makes you feel better."

Cypress rubs his head on her, almost pushing her over. She turns to the others and nods for Carmen to lead the way. Carmen grabs Julia's free hand and drags her along as he runs to the castle. Julia tries to steady her hand as they run so she can keep Cypress concealed. Illiana stumbles as she tries to maintain contact with Cypress and hold all her bags. His legs are longer than hers, allowing him to move quicker. As they approach the castle, everyone but Carmen slows. Their eyes light up with amazement. The castle is massive, with tall, towering peaks. There are bright blue flags with a gold A on them wave in the breeze. They admire the large stones making up the walls larger than Cypress. Carmen gets to the castle's front doors, frantically waving them over. The pathway leads to a wide staircase that stretches to the door. The stairs are split in half, with a waterfall running down the middle connecting to a stream. Julia's eyes follow it.

"Guys, come on, you'll have plenty of time to explore."

They all race up the steps, catching up with him.

"Welcome Home, everyone." Carmen turns and shoves open the doors. He grabs Julia's hand as he shouts through the Great Hall.

"Dad, where are you? Dad!"

A stampede of footsteps echoes in the hall. Carmen walks in, dragging Julia to the large staircase at the back of the room. Her gaze runs wild with amazement. The ceiling is high with two large crystal chandeliers hanging to extenuate the light throughout the room. There are three large doors on each side. Each door has a long blue cloth that hangs over the top, draping down the sides. Each piece of fabric is stitched with gold lettering and labeled for each room. Kitchen, Library, Garden, Wash Room, Parlor, Dining Hall. As the gallops of footsteps grow closer, she follows the blue carpet that flows up the grand stairway. Carmen's dad appears at the top of the stairs; his eyes widen as he pants out of breath.

"SON, IS THAT REALLY YOU?" the King screams as he runs down the stairs. Carmen meets him at the bottom of the steps. They fling their arms around each other as the two sob. The King pulls Carmen back, looking at his face. "Where have you been? You've been gone for weeks! I never thought I would see you again." Carmen's heart sinks with the word "weeks." He pulls him back in for a hug as Carmen pulls away.

"WEEKS? It's only been a week, Dad. It's hard to explain, and I have lots to tell you, but-"

"No, son, it's been SEVEN LONG WEEKS! We looked everywhere for you. We saw the unsealed door but couldn't open it to look for you. The others were starting to lose hope."

Carmen sighs, knowing that the time difference between universes is as he expected.

"Anyway, I am so happy you're home. Please tell me who our guest may be."

Carmen jumps back, running over to the others. "Dad, this is Julia, Illiana, and Cypress. I would like them to be part of our family here. They helped me get home, and I would really like it if they could stay."

The king half smiles as he only sees two people. He hurries over to Julia, extending a hand. She lowers her hand to shake his. The King gasps and pulls back. He falls to the floor, kicking his way back to the stairs. Julia looks at him, confused, as she holds out her hand. Carmen does a double-take as he realizes what his father is seeing.

"Dad, Dad, it's alright. This is Cypress. He is part of the family as well. I promise he won't hurt you."

Cypress lowers his head to the ground and walks over to the King. He is slow and gentle with his movements. The King hesitantly reaches out his shaky hand. Cypress pushes his head into his hand and starts purring. The King smiles, still shaking from his panic. Cypress lets out a squeal and starts licking the King's face. The King pulls back, scared again.

"Cypress, calm down, buddy. You gotta be slow at first; people need to get used to you." Carmen walks over, pulling Cypress back so he can help his father off the floor. "He's still young, so he gets a little over-excited."

The King nods as he reaches his hand out to Cypress again. Cypress approaches him slowly, placing his forehead against the King's hand. He closes his eyes and pushes memories to him. The King's eyes widen as he watches and listens.

"What, what, what is this? What is happening to me?"

Carmen chuckles as he places a hand on his father's shoulder. *"Cypress is nonverbal. This is how he communicates."*

The King smiles as Cypress flashes through various memories from their journey. The King's eyes twitch as his mind and ears are filled with memories.

"Well, I guess he's filled me in pretty well for the most part. You are all more than welcome to stay; our home is your home. After all, we're all family." He leans over to wink at Julia. Her cheeks turn red as she blushes with embarrassment. He pulls his hand back quickly from Cypress, still a little shaken. *"Why don't we all settle down for lunch, and you can tell me more? Oh, and please do not hide Cypress. I will find great joy in everyone's panic as they meet him for the first time."* The King

laughs as he pushes open the large door to the dining hall. Cypress and Illiana rush in for a feast. The King and Carmen chuckle together as they can hear the screams of the kitchen staff getting their first sight of Cypress.

Julia walks over, wrapping an arm around Carmen. The King takes her hand to greet her properly this time. She bows slightly as she shakes his hand. He pulls her in, hugging her tightly. Her eyes widen as she slams into him, hugging him back. He feels welcoming, just like Carmen. "Please keep my boy close. You have great strength, and he will need you." He whispers quietly in her ear before pulling back. Julia nods with a big smile, her cheeks flush with embarrassment.

There is a loud bang at the top of the stairs, and everyone jolts, looking up.

"Who are these people in our castle, Tobias? You know I don't like unexpected guests in our home."

The King sighs as he rolls his eyes at the tall, lanky woman at the top of the stairs. She has on a long silk robe with fur stitched to the ends. Her graying hair is styled in a large bun. Carmen follows his father, rolling his eyes as she slowly descends the stairs. Julia catches his eye roll and gently smacks his shoulder. She gives the women a small wave and courtesy. The woman sticks her nose higher in the air.

"Elenora, must you always make a dramatic entrance? Carmen is home; my boy is here!"

Her face remains unsurprised as she continues down the stairs with her nose up.

"Ah, I can see that with my own two eyes Tobias. I'm not blind. Carmen, we thought you were dead. I can see we were mistaken." Her voice is arrogant and posh. Carmen rolls his eyes again, flinching, expecting another smack from Julia. This time, she glares at her angrily.

"Nope, very much alive, Elenora. Just needed to take a journey of discovery."

Elenora raises an eyebrow at him, still keeping her nose high.

"First, I am your aunt, and you will address me as such. Second, I hope your journey of self-discovery was worth it because you caused quite a stir in the villages. People were worried about the future with the future King presumed dead."

Carmen huffs at her as she holds a limp hand out as if looking to be assisted down the last step. She scoffs as no one moves to her aid.

"Well, they can be reassured that I am home safe now and will resume my duties to become their next king."

Elanora throws her head back with a high-pitched hearty laugh. "Your cousin Jeff has already eased the villagers' worries. Someone needed to calm them in your absence. See, while you abandoned them, he made a daily presence to show he would not. As I stated before, I hope your journey of self-discovery was worth it because it cost you your kingdom."